THE

**MILLS & BOON**

# Summer Short Stories Collection

**Celebrate the summer with Mills & Boon!
Enjoy three classic short stories from
your favourite authors – the perfect little
indulgence for a summer's day!**

All the characters in this book have no existence outside the imagination of
the author, and have no relation whatsoever to anyone bearing the same name
or names. They are not even distantly inspired by any individual known or
unknown to the author, and all the incidents are pure invention.

Harlequin Mills & Boon Limited,
Eton House, 18-24 Paradise Road, Richmond, Surrey, TW9 1SR

The Sheikh's Virgin © Susan Macias Redmond 2002

ISBN: 978 0 263 86736 7

077-0809

Harlequin Mills & Boon policy is to use papers that are natural, renewable
and recyclable products and made from wood grown in sustainable forests.
The logging and manufacturing processes conform to the legal environmental
regulations of the country of origin.

Printed and bound in Spain
by Litografia Rosés S.A., Barcelona

# The Sheikh's Virgin

## SUSAN MALLERY

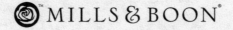

**Susan Mallery** is the bestselling author of over thirty-five books for Mills & Boon. Best known for combining humour with emotion and creating extraordinary characters who live on in the imagination, Susan publishes five or six books each year.

Susan is married and lives with her husband in sunny Southern California where the weather is always perfect and the eccentricities of a writer are considered almost normal. She has two beautiful but not very bright cats, and the world's greatest stepson.

# Chapter 1

The island of Lucia-Serrat glittered like an emerald in a bed of sapphires. Phoebe Carson pressed her forehead against the window of the small commuter plane and stared at the lush landscape below. As they circled in preparation for landing, she saw a snow-white beach, a rain forest, a crescent of blue, blue ocean, then a small city perched on a cliff. Her heart pounded in her chest and her ears popped.

The flight attendant announced that it was time to return seat backs and tray tables to their upright positions. What had seemed so strange when her journey had begun was second nature to her now. Phoebe tightened her seat belt and checked her tray table. She'd been too busy staring out the window to bother putting her seat back. She'd wanted to see everything as they approached Lucia-Serrat.

''Just as you promised, Ayanna,'' she whispered to herself. ''So beautiful. Thank you for allowing me to spend this time here.''

Phoebe returned her attention to the view out the window. The ground seemed to rush up to meet them, then she felt the gentle bump of the airplane wheels on the runway. She could see lush trees and bushes, tropical flowers and brightly colored birds. Then the plane turned to taxi toward the terminal and her view of paradise was lost.

Thirty minutes later Phoebe had collected her small suitcase and passed through customs and immigration. The official-looking young man had greeted her, stamped her passport and had asked if she had anything to declare. When she said she did not, he waved her through.

As easy as that, Phoebe thought, tucking her crisp new passport into her handbag.

All around her families greeted each other, while young couples, obviously on their honeymoon, strolled slowly arm in arm. Phoebe felt a little alone, but she refused to be lonely. Not at the beginning of her adventure. She found the courtesy phone and called her hotel. The hotel clerk promised that the driver would arrive to pick her up within fifteen minutes.

Phoebe had started for the glass doors leading out of the airport when a small store window caught her eye. She didn't usually shop very much, but the display drew her. Bottles of French perfume sat in nests of satin. Designer handbags and shoes hung on barely visible wires from the ceiling of the display case. Everything looked beautiful and very expensive, yet she knew there was no harm in looking while she waited for her ride to the hotel.

Phoebe stepped into the coolness of the store and inhaled a cloud of perfume-scented air. Different fragrances blended together perfectly. Although she was intrigued by the bottles on display, the tall, chicly dressed woman behind the counter made her nervous, so she turned in the opposite direction, only to find herself in front of a case of jewelry.

Rings, earrings, bracelets and necklaces appeared to have been casually tossed into the velvet-lined case. Yet Phoebe suspected it took a long time to make everything look so artless. She bent to get a closer look. One of the center diamonds in a cocktail ring was larger than the nail on her little finger. Phoebe figured she could probably live well for a couple of years on what that one piece cost. If this was an example of shopping in Lucia-Serrat, she would restrict hers to looking in windows.

"I think that is too large for you."

The unexpected comment caught her off guard. She straightened immediately, pressing her hand to her chest.

"I was just looking," she said breathlessly. "I didn't touch anything."

A man stood in front of her. While she was tall— nearly five-ten—he was several inches taller. Dark

hair had been brushed back from his handsome face.
There were tiny lines by the corners of his amazing
brown-black eyes, and a hint of a smile teasing at the
corners of his mouth. She told herself to look away—
that it was rude to stare—but something about his
expression, or maybe it was the sculptured lines of
his cheekbones and jaw, compelled her.

He looked like a male model in an expensive liquor
ad, only a little older. Phoebe instantly felt out of
place and foolish. Her dress had cost less than twenty
dollars at a discount outlet, and that had been last
year, while the man's suit looked really expensive.
Not that she had a lot of experience with things like
men's suits.

"The bracelet," he said.

She blinked at him. "Excuse me?"

"I thought you were looking at the sapphire bracelet. While it's lovely and the color of the stones
matches your eyes, it is too large for your delicate
wrist. Several links would have to be removed."

She forced herself to tear her gaze from his face,
and looked at the jewelry case. Right in the center
was a sapphire bracelet. Oval blue stones surrounded
by diamonds. It probably cost more than a beachfront
hotel back home in Florida.

"It's very nice," she said politely.

"Ah, you do not like it."

"No. I mean yes, of course I like it. It's beautiful."
But wishing after something like that was about as
realistic as expecting to buy a 747.

"Perhaps there was something else you were shopping for?"

"No. Just looking."

She risked glancing at him again. There was something about his dark eyes, something almost…kind. Which made no sense. Handsome gentlemen didn't notice women like her. Actually no one noticed women like her. She was too tall, too thin and much too plain. Nor had anyone ever made her stomach flutter as it was doing right now.

"Is this your first visit to Lucia-Serrat?" he asked.

Phoebe thought of the blank pages in her new passport. "It's my first trip anywhere," she confessed. "I'd never been on a plane until this morning." She frowned as she thought about the time zones she'd crossed. "Or maybe it was yesterday. I flew from Miami to New York, then to Bahania, then to here."

He raised one eyebrow. "I see. Forgive me for saying this, but Lucia-Serrat seems an unusual place to begin one's travels. Many people are not familiar with the island. Although it is very beautiful."

"Very," she agreed. "I haven't seen very much. I mean, I just arrived, but I saw it from the plane window. I thought it looked like an emerald. So green and glittering in the middle of the ocean." She inhaled deeply. "It even smells different. Florida is sort of tropical, but nothing like this. Everyone seems so cosmopolitan and sure of themselves. I don't even know what—"

She pressed her lips together and ducked her head.

"Sorry," she murmured, wondering if she could have sounded more like a schoolgirl. "I didn't mean to blurt all that out."

"Do not apologize. I am enjoying your enthusiasm."

There was something about the cadence of his speech, Phoebe thought dreamily. His English was perfect, but had a more formal quality. There was also a trace of an accent, not that she could place it.

He lightly touched her chin, as if requesting she raise her head. The contact was fleeting at best, and yet she felt the impact all the way down to her toes.

"What brings you to my island?" he asked gently.

"You live here?"

"All of my life." He hesitated, then shrugged. "My family has been in residence for over five hundred years. We came for the spices and stayed for the oil."

"Oh, my." That sounded so romantic. "I, um, wanted to visit because of a family member. My great-aunt was born here. She always talked about the island and how she hated to leave. She passed away a few months ago." Some of Phoebe's happiness bled away as a pang of loneliness shot through her. "She wanted me to see the world, but it was her request that I begin here, where she was born."

"You and your great-aunt were close?"

Phoebe leaned against the jewelry case. From the corner of her eye she saw two store clerks talking frantically in the corner. They gestured wildly, but didn't approach either her or the stranger.

"She raised me," she said, returning her attention to the kind man in front of her. "I never knew my father, and my mother died when I was eight. Great-Aunt Ayanna took me in." She smiled at the memory. "I'd been raised in Colorado, so moving to Florida was pretty exciting. Ayanna said it was the closest place to Lucia-Serrat she could find. I think she missed the island very much."

"So you honor her memory by visiting the island."

Phoebe hadn't thought of it that way. She smiled. "That's exactly right. I want to visit the places she liked to go. She even gave me a list."

The tall stranger held out his hand. Obviously he wanted to read the list. Phoebe reached into the outside pocket of her purse and handed it to him.

He unfolded the single sheet of paper and read silently. She took the opportunity to study his thick hair and the length of his lashes, the powerful build of his body. They weren't standing very close at all, yet she would swear she felt the heat of his body. A crazy thing to be thinking, she told herself. But true. A warmth seeped through her as she watched him.

As he returned the list to her, he said, "All excellent choices. Are you familiar with the legend of Lucia's Point?"

Phoebe had long since memorized Ayanna's list. Lucia's Point was second from the bottom. "Not at all."

"They say that only lovers may visit. If they make love in the shade of the waterfall, they will be blessed all the days of their lives. So have you brought your lover with you?"

Phoebe suspected he was teasing her, but she couldn't stop herself from blushing. A lover? Couldn't the man tell from looking at her that she'd never even had a boyfriend, let alone a lover?

Before she could think of something to say—preferably something witty and charming and sophisticated—a uniformed man appeared at her side.

"Ms. Phoebe Carson? I am here to take you to your hotel." He bowed slightly and took her luggage. "At your convenience," he said, and backed out of the store.

Phoebe glanced out the window and saw a green van sitting at the curb. Gold lettering spelled out Parrot Bay Inn, where she would be staying for the next month.

"My ride is here," she told the stranger who had lingered to chat with her.

"I can see. I hope you will enjoy your time in Lucia-Serrat."

His dark eyes seemed to see inside her. Could he read her mind? She hoped not—if he could, he would figure out that she was an inexperienced fool who was completely out of her element with him.

"You've been very kind," she murmured when nothing more charming occurred to her.

"My pleasure."

Before she could turn away, he reached out and took her hand in his, then raised it to chest level. He bent his head and lightly kissed her fingers. The old-world gesture took her breath away, as did the tingling that instantly shot up her arm.

"Perhaps we will be lucky enough to run into each other again," he said.

Phoebe was incapable of speech. Fortunately he left before she did something really embarrassing like stutter or babble. After a couple of seconds she was able to draw in a breath. Then she forced herself to start walking. She left the store and stepped out into the warm afternoon. It was only when she was settled in the hotel van that she thought to look for the man she'd met in the store. She didn't even know his name.

But look as she might, she couldn't spot him. The driver climbed in and started the engine. Five minutes later they had left the airport behind them and were on a two-lane road that hugged a cliff above the sea.

The ocean stretched out to the horizon on her right, while on her left, lush foliage crept down to the side of the road. Flashes of color fluttered from branch to branch, proof of the wild parrots that made their home on the tropical island. Phoebe could smell that salty air and the rich, dark earth dampened by a recent shower. Excitement coursed through her—she was really here, she thought as the van arrived at the hotel.

The Parrot Bay Inn had been built nearly two hundred years before. The white building soared up sev-

eral stories, with red and pink bougainvilleas covering
the bottom two floors. The foyer was an open atrium,
the reception desk hand carved with an elegance from
an older time. Phoebe registered and was shown to
her room.

Ayanna had made her niece promise to visit the
island of Lucia-Serrat for a month, and to stay only
at the Parrot Bay Inn. Phoebe refused to consider the
expense as she was shown to a lovely corner mini-
suite complete with a view of the ocean and a balcony
worthy of Romeo and Juliet. She felt as if she were
floating as she stepped out to watch the sun sink toward the west.

A reddish-orange bath colored the sky. The water
turned from blue to dark green. She breathed in the
scents of the island as she leaned against her balcony
railing and savored the moment.

When it was dark, she moved back into her room
to unpack and settle in for her stay. The four-poster
bed looked comfortable and the bathroom, while old-
fashioned, was large and contained every amenity. If
the silence made her a little sad, she refused to dwell
on her loneliness. She was used to making her own
way. Here, on the island of her great-aunt's birth, she
would connect with all that Ayanna had spoken of.
She would feel her aunt's presence. She would begin
to live her life.

Just before she went down to dinner there was a
knock on her door. When she opened it, a bellman
carried in a large spray of tropical flowers, touched

his cap and left before Phoebe could tell him there must be some mistake. No one would be sending her flowers.

Even though she knew it was foolish, she couldn't help imagining the handsome stranger she'd met at the duty-free shop at the airport. No. Not him. He had to be at least thirty-three or thirty-four. He would think of her as a child, nothing more. Yet her fingers trembled as she opened the white envelope tucked among the blossoms.

"May your stay on the island be delightful."

No signature. Which meant that while they weren't from the man at the store, she could pretend they were. She could imagine that instead of awkward, she'd been funny and charming. Instead of dressed in something old and out of style, she'd been elegant and sophisticated and that he couldn't stop thinking about her. Much as she couldn't stop thinking about him.

The next morning Phoebe took the stairs instead of the elevator. She wore loose cotton trousers and sandals, a tank top covered by a matching short-sleeved shirt. While Lucia-Serrat was more forward thinking than many Arab countries, she didn't want to cause offense by dressing too immodestly. In her oversize straw bag she'd packed sunscreen, a few pieces of fruit from the bowl in her room, a bottle of water and a map. Today she would begin to tackle Ayanna's list, beginning with what was closest to the hotel.

When she grew more familiar with her way, she would rent a car and explore the outlying areas. As for visiting Lucia's Point, well, she would deal with that problem when she had to.

Phoebe skipped down the last two steps and stepped into the foyer of the hotel.

"Good morning. I trust you slept well?"

She skittered to a stop, unable to believe what she was seeing. It was him—the man from the store the previous day. Oh, the suit was gone, replaced by casual trousers and a crisp white shirt. But she recognized his handsome features and the odd fluttering in her stomach. His teeth flashed white as he smiled at her.

"I see by your expression of surprise that you remember me. I hope the memory is pleasant."

She thought of how she'd gone to sleep remembering his light kiss on her fingers, and her dreams of a dark-haired stranger promising to show her the delights of Lucia's Point. A blush crawled up her face.

"Good morning," she whispered, thinking that response was a whole lot safer than discussing her memories of him.

"So you begin your tour of my island today. I remember—your aunt's list. What did you wish to explore first?"

Phoebe didn't know what to say. "I thought I would start with the Parrot Cove beach," she said hesitantly, not sure what brought him to the hotel, or why he bothered to speak with her. While thoughts of him had kept her occupied for hours last night, she couldn't have been a very interesting encounter for him.

"Not the beach," he said with a flick of his wrist. "While we have the most beautiful beaches in the world on the island, there is nothing extraordinary about sand. I have decided we will start with the banyan tree."

Phoebe resisted the urge to stick her finger in her ear to see if something was stuck there. She couldn't possibly have heard the man correctly. "I, um…" She took a deep breath. "I don't understand."

"Then I need to be more clear. I was charmed by what you told me yesterday and I have decided to assist you in fulfilling your late aunt's last request. Therefore I shall escort you to all the places on the list." He gave her a rakish smile. "Well, perhaps not *all* the places."

She instantly thought of Lucia's Point, which was no doubt what he wanted her to do. She thought the man might actually be teasing her. Was it possible? No one ever took the time to kid around with her.

And as tempting as his offer might be, there were a couple of things she couldn't forget. "I wouldn't want to be a bother, and even if you were willing to share your time with me, we've only just met. I don't even know your name."

He touched his fingertips lightly to his chest. "I am most remiss," he said, and swept her a low bow. He should have looked silly, but somehow he managed to look very elegant. "I am Mazin, a resident of the island, and your servant for as long as you command me to serve."

Phoebe couldn't believe this was happening—maybe in a movie, but not in real life and certainly not to her. She glanced around and realized that everyone in the lobby was watching them. She hesitated, torn between what she wanted to do and what she knew she *must* do.

"Miss Carson?" A man approached. The brass name tag said he was Mr. Eldon, the hotel manager. "I want to assure you that, ah…" He glanced at the stranger. "That Mazin is a most honorable gentleman. No harm will come to you while you are in his presence."

"You see," Mazin said. "I have those who are willing to vouch for my character. Come, Phoebe. See the wonders of Lucia-Serrat with me."

She was about to refuse—because she prided herself on being sensible—when Ayanna's words came back to her. Her aunt had wanted her to live life to the fullest and never have regrets. Phoebe knew she would regret refusing Mazin's invitation, regardless of how foolish it might be to accept.

"The banyan tree sounds very nice," she said softly, and allowed Mazin to lead her out to his waiting car.

# Chapter 2

The young woman cast one last tentative glance over her shoulder before slipping into the front seat of his Mercedes. Mazin closed the door and circled to the driver's side, all the while trying to figure out what he was doing.

He didn't have time to play games with children—and that's exactly what Phoebe Carson was. A child of twenty or so. Far too young and inexperienced to succeed at his kind of game. Why was he bothering? Worse, why was he wasting his time?

He slid onto the driver's seat and glanced at her.

She stared at him, her eyes wide—as if she were a cornered rabbit and he were some deadly predator. A perfect metaphor, he thought wryly. He should walk away—tell her that he was too busy to take her on a tour of the island. If he wanted a woman—*a woman,* not a child—there were dozens who would fly to his side at the first hint of his interest. They knew him and his world. They knew what was expected. They understood the rules.

Phoebe understood nothing. Even as he put the car in gear, he knew he was making a mistake. Because he was acting against his good sense—something he never allowed himself to do. His nature didn't allow him to take advantage of those who were not his equal. So why was he here with her?

Yesterday he had seen her going through customs. She had seemed both brave and terrified…and very much an innocent. At first he had kept track of her because he had been sure she was being met and he wanted to make sure she found her way. Later, when he had realized she was alone, he had found himself compelled to approach her for reasons he could not explain.

He had just returned from his own trip abroad. He should have been eager to go home. And yet he had taken the time to speak with Phoebe. Having spoken with her, he could not forget her.

Madness, he told himself. Simple madness.

''The weather seems very nice,'' she said, interrupting his thoughts.

Mazin glanced out the front windshield. The sky was blue and cloudless. ''With only the occasional sprinkle, this is our dry season,'' he told her. ''In the fall we have a rainy season, followed by several weeks of monsoons. Sometimes I am surprised that all of Lucia-Serrat doesn't wash away into the sea. But we survive and after the rains, everything grows.''

Maybe it was her eyes, he thought as he turned onto the main road. So wide and blue. Trusting, he thought grimly. She was far too trusting. No one could be that innocent. He gritted his teeth. Was that the problem? Did he think she was pretending?

He wasn't sure. Did women like her really exist, or was this all an elaborate plot to get close to him? He glanced at her, taking in the long blond hair pulled back in a thick braid and her simple, inexpensive clothing. Was she trying to put him at his ease by appearing so far out of his league as to be beneath notice? Yet he had noticed. For reasons he could not explain, she intrigued him.

So he would play her game—whatever that might be—until he learned the truth, or grew tired of her. Because he would grow tired…he always did.

''You said your family had been here five hundred years,'' she said, glancing at him quickly, then returning her attention to the window. ''I can't imagine having that much personal history.''

''The island was first discovered by explorers setting out from Bahania nearly a thousand years ago,'' he told her. ''It was uninhabited and considered sacred ground. The royal family claimed it for their own. As European sailors set out to conquer the New World, the king of Bahania grew concerned that his private paradise would be taken for Portugal, Spain or England. So he sent relatives to live here. Eventually the island became populated. A sovereignty was established. To this day, the crown prince of the island is a cousin of the king of Bahania.''

Phoebe looked at him, her eyes wide. ''I guess I knew about there being a prince, because that's how my great-aunt got in trouble, but I never thought about there being one right this minute. Does he live on the island?''

''Yes, he is a permanent resident.''

She looked as if she were about to ask another question, when they drove past a break in the trees. Phoebe stared at the view of the ocean and caught her breath.

''It's so beautiful.''

''Do you not see the ocean where you live?''

''Sometimes.'' She gave him a quick smile before returning her attention to the view. ''Ayanna's house is a few miles inland. I used to spend a lot of time by the water when I was in school, but after she became ill, I never had the time.''

She pressed her fingers against the window. Her hands were as delicate as the rest of her. Mazin eyed her clothes. They were worn, although well cared for. In the right designer gown, with a little makeup and her hair styled, she would be a beauty. Like this, she was a plain gray dove.

While the fantasy of Phoebe as a femme fatale appealed to him, he found himself equally attracted to the little dove sitting next to him.

A dove who had no idea of his identity. Perhaps that was part of her appeal. He so rarely spent time with women who were not clear on who he was and what he could give them.

"There is a grove of spice trees," he said, pointing to his left. "People assume that spices come from seeds, but often they are found in the tree bark."

She turned to look. As she leaned toward his side of the car, he caught the scent of her body. Soap, he thought, nearly smiling. She smelled of the rose soap left for guests at the Parrot Bay Inn.

"Dozens of different kinds of spice are grown here," he said.

"What are those flowers?" she asked. "Are they growing out of the tree bark?"

"No. They're orchids. They're grafted into the branches of the trees and grown for use in flower arrangements. Some are used in perfume. Mango trees are the best hosts, but you will find orchids growing everywhere on the island."

"I haven't seen any oil pumps. You said there was oil on the island. Or is it out at sea?"

"Both."

He waited, wondering if this was where she would tip her hand. Interest in oil meant interest in money…specifically his. But Phoebe didn't even blink. She turned her attention to the passenger window, almost as if the oil didn't matter.

Now that he thought about it he realized that her enthusiasm for the island was far greater than her enthusiasm for him accompanying her. Was she really the shy tourist she claimed to be?

He couldn't remember the last time a woman hadn't hung on to his every word. It was almost as if she wasn't overly interested in what he had to say. If true, it was a unique experience.

They rounded a bend. The main bazaar stretched out on a flat stretch of stone-covered earth.

"The Lucia-Serrat marketplace has been in existence for nearly five hundred years," he said. "These outer walls are part of the original walls that surrounded the area."

Phoebe clapped her hands together in delight. "Oh, Mazin, we must stop. Look at everything they're selling. Those little copper pots and flowers and oh, is that a monkey?"

She laughed as a small monkey climbed across several open-air booths to snatch a particularly ripe slice of mango from a display. The owner of the monkey handed over a coin before the owner of the fruit stall could complain.

Mazin shook his head. "Not today, Phoebe. We will save the bazaar for another day. After all, you have a list and to see everything, we must proceed in an orderly fashion."

"Of course. Your way makes sense." She leaned back in her seat. "I've always been in favor of being orderly." She sighed softly. "Except something about this island makes me want to be reckless.'' She smiled at him. "I am not, by nature, a reckless person.''

''I see.''

Her innocent words, the light in her eyes and the way her smile lingered on her full mouth sent a jolt of desire through him. The arousal was so unexpected, Mazin almost didn't recognize it at first.

He wanted her. He *wanted* her. How long had it been since he had done little more than go through the motions of making love? His desire had faded until he could barely remember what it was like to ache with passion. He had bedded the most skilled, the most beautiful women of his acquaintance and none of them had stirred him beyond the desire necessary to perform. Yet here, with this plain gray dove, he felt heat for the first time in years.

The fates that determined his life were once again having a great laugh at his expense.

''What do you know of present-day Lucia-Serrat?'' he asked.

''Not very much. Ayanna mostly talked about the past. What it was like when she was my age.'' Her expression softened with obvious affection. ''She would describe glittering parties she attended. Apparently she was invited to the prince's private residence for several events. She talked about meeting visiting dignitaries from other countries. She even met the Prince of Wales—the one who became King Edward and then abdicated the throne for Mrs. Simpson. Ayanna said he was an elegant dancer.''

She talked about other parties her great-aunt had attended. Mazin wasn't sure if her lack of knowledge about current events on Lucia-Serrat was real or pretense. If she played a game, she played it well. If not—

He didn't want to think about that. If Phoebe Carson was exactly what she appeared to be, he had no business involving himself with her. He was jaded and far too old. Unfortunately, with his body unexpectedly hard with desire, he doubted he was noble enough to walk away.

"Look," Mazin said, pointing out the window. "There are parrots in the trees."

Phoebe strained to see, then rolled down her window. The tall trees were alive with the colorful birds. Reds, greens, blues all blended together into a fluttering rainbow of activity. She breathed in the sweet air of the island and thought how it was a miracle that she was here at all.

Mazin turned left, heading inland. Mazin. Phoebe still couldn't believe that he'd actually come to her hotel that morning simply to show her around the island and help her with Ayanna's list. Men never noticed her. It was amazing enough that he'd bothered to speak with her yesterday, but to have remembered her through the night—who would have thought it possible?

She brushed her hands against her slacks. Her

palms were damp. Nerves, she thought. She'd never met anyone like Mazin. He was so sophisticated and worldly. He made her nervous.

A sign up ahead caught her attention. A carving of a small creature standing on its back feet and staring toward the sky sat on top of the sign.

"Meerkats," she breathed. "Oh, look. It's the reserve."

"I suppose you're going to ask me to stop there, as well."

She wanted to, but thought the banyan tree was a better outing to share with her companion. At least staring at a tree wouldn't make her babble like an idiot. Being around adorable meerkats with their funny faces and charming antics would make her gush in a very embarrassing way.

"I'm determined to abide by the schedule," she said, trying to sound mature. "I'll see the meerkats another day."

"Quite sensible," Mazin murmured.

His tone of voice caught her attention. She glanced at him, taking in his strong profile and the air of confidence and power that surrounded him. She didn't know why he bothered with her, but she knew that whatever his expectations, he was destined to be disappointed. She had never been good at fitting in. She had no experience with the opposite sex—not that he was interested in her that way.

"You probably think of me as a child," she said before she could stop herself. Heat instantly flared on her cheeks and she had to resist the need to bury her face in her hands. Instead she pretended to be engrossed in the view out the passenger window.

"A child," he repeated. "Not that. A young woman. How old are you, Phoebe?"

She thought about lying, making herself sound older, but what was the point? People already thought she was much younger than her actual age.

"I'm twenty-three."

"So very grown-up," he teased.

She glanced at him. Their eyes met and she was relieved when she saw his expression was kind. "I'm not all that grown-up. I've seen little of the world, but what I have seen has taught me to depend on myself." She swallowed, then risked asking a question of her own. "How old are you?"

"Thirty-seven."

She did the math instantly. Fourteen years. Not such an impossible distance, although she didn't know what Mazin would think of it. No doubt his world was incredibly different from hers. They would have no experiences in common—which might make the age difference seem even larger.

Not that it mattered, she reminded herself. She didn't know why he'd taken time out of his day to show her around the island, but she doubted he had any *personal* interest in her.

She briefly wondered if he'd ever been married, but before she could gather the courage to ask, he turned down a narrow road. Trees and shrubs grew on both sides, their bright green leaves nearly brushing against the sides of the car.

"The banyan tree is protected by royal decree," Mazin said as he pulled into an empty parking lot. "It is considered a national treasure."

"A tree?"

"We value that which is unique to our island."

His low voice seemed to brush across her skin. Phoebe shivered slightly as she stepped out of his car. She glanced back once, noticing for the first time that he drove a *large* Mercedes. She recognized the symbol on the hood, but had no idea about the type of car, save that it was big and a silvery gray. Back home she drove a nine-year-old Honda.

Different worlds, she thought again.

"Is the park open?" she asked as they headed for a path leading to a covered patio with an information booth at the far end. She glanced both left and right. "There isn't anyone else around."

"This is not our busy season for tourists," Mazin told her as he lightly touched the back of her arm to guide her up the stairs toward the information booth. "Plus it is early in the day for visitors. However, the park is open."

Phoebe studied the plants they passed. She didn't know any of them on sight. There were brightly colored blossoms everywhere. Lavender star-shaped flowers hung from spindly trees. Spine-covered pods in vivid red reached for the sun. A wild and sultry perfume filled the air as if the flowers conspired to intoxicate her. Even the air brushed against her body like a sensual caress. Lucia-Serrat was like no place she had ever been.

Mazin reached the information booth. He spoke quietly with the person inside. Phoebe glanced up and saw that the price of admission was three local dollars. She reached for the purse she'd slung over her shoulder, then hesitated. What was she supposed to do? It hadn't occurred to her that Mazin would pay, but would he be mad if she said anything?

She had barely fumbled with the zipper on her purse when he turned and looked at her. His dark eyes narrowed.

"Do not even consider insulting me, my dove."

There was steel behind his words. Phoebe nodded and dropped her hands to her side. Then she replayed his sentence, pausing at the very end. *My dove.* It didn't mean anything, she told herself as she mentally stumbled over the two words. No man had ever called her by anything other than her name. But it wasn't significant. He probably used flowery language with everyone.

She would store this memory away, she told herself. Later, when she was alone, she would pull it out and pretend that he had meant something wonderful. It would be a harmless game, something to hold the loneliness at bay.

He collected two tickets and they walked through an arch covered with blossoming bougainvillea.

"People think the pink and red on bougainvillea

are the flowers,'' Phoebe said inanely before she
could stop herself. ''Actually those are just leaves.
The flowers are very small and often white.''

''You know horticulture?'' Mazin asked.

''Uh, not really. Just that. I read about it somewhere. I read a lot of things. I guess my head is full
of obscure facts. I could probably do well on a game
show.''

She consciously pressed her lips together to keep
from talking. Could she sound more stupid? The fact
that Mazin made her nervous was of interest to no
one save herself. If she continued to act like an idiot,
he wasn't going to want to spend any more time with
her.

The stone path had been worn smooth by years of
use. They stepped from bright sun into shade provided by large trees. There were several formal gar-
dens all around them. As they turned a corner, Phoebe
caught her breath. In front of them stood the famous
Lucia-Serrat banyan tree.

From where they were standing, they couldn't see
the center of the tree. Branches spread out in all di-
rections, some slender, some as thick around as a
man. Sturdy roots grew down from the branches, an-
choring the tree to the ground in hundreds of places.
The tree itself stretched out for what seemed like
miles. A small sign said that the circumference of the
aerial roots was nearly ten acres.

''Is it the biggest in the world?'' she asked.

"No. There is a larger tree in India. There is also a large one in Hawaii, although this one is bigger."

The leaves were huge and oval, tapering on each end. She stepped forward, ducking under several branches. There were paths through the aerial root system. She could see where others had walked. Reverently she touched the surprisingly smooth bark. This tree had been alive for hundreds of years.

"It feels like it's a living part of the structure of the island," she said, glancing back at Mazin.

He shrugged. "There is strength in the tree. Once it gets established, it can survive most any kind of storm. Even if one part is destroyed, the rest survives."

"I wouldn't mind being that strong," she said as she crouched down and picked up a fallen leaf.

"Why would you think you are not?"

She glanced at him. He stood within the shade of the tree. His dark eyes were unreadable. Phoebe suddenly realized she knew nothing about this man, that she was on a strange island and for all she knew, he made a habit of abducting female tourists traveling alone. She should be cautious and wary.

Yet she didn't want to be. Whatever had drawn her to Mazin continued to pull her to him today. She was foolish to trust him, and yet trust him she did.

"Strength requires experience and knowledge," she said. "I haven't lived very much. I never made it to college." She rose to her feet, still clutching the leaf in her hand. "My aunt got sick the summer after

I graduated from high school. She wanted me to go live my life, but I stayed home to take care of her.''

She rubbed the leaf between her fingers, then dropped it to the ground. "I'm not complaining. I don't have any regrets. I loved Ayanna and would give up everything to have her with me again. I would rather be with her now than be here or—"

Phoebe broke off when she realized what she'd said. Embarrassment gripped her. "I'm sorry. I didn't mean to imply that I wasn't enjoying your company."

Mazin dismissed her apology with a wave of his hand. "It is of no concern. I am not insulted. Your affection for your aunt does you credit."

He stared at her as if she were some strange creature he'd never seen before. Phoebe touched her cheek with the back of her hand and hoped the shadows of the tree kept him from seeing how she blushed. No doubt he found her silly and boring.

"Are you hungry?" he asked abruptly. "There is a café nearby. I thought we could have lunch."

Her heart fluttered, her embarrassment fled and it was as if the sun brightened the sky a little more than it had. Mazin held out his hand in invitation. Phoebe hesitated only a second before placing her trembling fingers in his hand.

# Chapter 3

The café sat on the edge of the ocean. Phoebe felt as if she could stretch out her foot and touch the blue water. A soft breeze carried the scent of salt and island flowers, perfuming the air. The sun was hot, yet a large umbrella shielded them so that they felt only pleasantly warm.

She had the strongest urge to bounce up and down with excitement. She couldn't believe she was really here, on the island, having lunch with a very handsome man. If this was a dream, she didn't ever want to wake up.

Mazin was being so very kind. Her fingers still tingled from his touch when he'd held her hand as they'd walked to his car. She knew he hadn't intended the gesture to have meaning. There was no way he could have known how the heat from his hand had burned into her skin or made her heart race so delightfully.

"Have you decided?" he asked.

She glanced at the menu she held and realized she hadn't read it. She'd been too busy admiring the view.

"Maybe there's a local dish you would like to recommend," she said.

"The fresh fish. The chef here prides himself on his preparation. You won't be disappointed."

As she knew she wouldn't be able to taste anything, she didn't doubt that he was right. He could feed her ground-up cardboard and she would be content.

Their waiter appeared and Mazin gave him their orders. Phoebe picked up her iced tea and took a sip.

"This is such a beautiful spot," she said as she put down her glass. "I'm surprised it's not crowded for lunch."

Mazin seemed to hesitate. "Sometimes it is, but we're a little early."

Phoebe glanced at her watch. It was nearly noon, but she wasn't about to contradict her host. Besides, it might be fashionable to dine late on the island.

They sat on a patio that held about a dozen tables, all protected by umbrellas. In the distance she could see a grove of trees filled with parrots. Small lizards sunned themselves on the stone wall across from their table.

"What do you think of my island?" Mazin asked.

She smiled with contentment. "It's beautiful.

Ayanna always talked about Lucia-Serrat being paradise, but I'm not sure I ever believed her. Everything is so clean. It's not just the absence of trash on the road, but the fact that plant life grows everywhere. Are there really other people on this island?"

He smiled. "I assure you, my dove, we are not alone."

Too bad, she thought wistfully.

"There has been much debate about the future of the island. We require certain resources to survive, yet we do not want to destroy the beauty that brightens our world."

"There's a lot of that kind of talk in Florida," Phoebe said, leaning forward slightly. "Developers want to build apartment buildings and hotels. They impact the infrastructure. Growth is good for the economy, but irresponsible growth can be bad for the land itself. It's a delicate balance. I worry about things like the rain forest. Part of me wants to come firmly on the side of whatever tree or animal is in need, but I know that people need to eat and heat their homes."

"I would have assumed you were a rabid conservationist," he said, his voice teasing.

She smiled. "I'm not the rabid type. I care and I do what I can. I don't think there are any easy answers."

"I agree. Here on Lucia-Serrat we seek to find a balance. We live in harmony with nature. Yes, we must dig for oil, but all precautions are taken to protect the sea and those creatures who live there. That adds to the cost. There are those who protest, who want more oil and less worry about the birds and the fish.'' His brows drew together. ''There are those who would influence policy, but so far I have been—''

He broke off in midsentence, then shrugged. ''So far I have been happy with the choices the prince has made.''

Phoebe rested her elbows on the table. ''Do you know the prince?''

''I am familiar with the royal family.''

She turned that over in her mind. It was hard to imagine. ''I've never even met the mayor where I live,'' she said, more to herself than to him. ''Don't you like him?''

Mazin's eyebrows rose in surprise. ''Why do you ask me that?''

''I don't know. The way you said you've been happy with his choices. There was something in your voice. I thought maybe you didn't like him.''

''I assure you, that is not the case.''

She sipped her iced tea. ''Is there a parliament or something to keep the prince in line? I mean, what if he started making unfair rules? Could anyone stop him?''

''Prince Nasri is a wise and honorable ruler. To answer your questions, there is a form of parliament. They handle much of the government, but the prince is the true leader of the people.''

''Is he well liked?''

''I believe so. He is considered just. Two days a

month anyone may come to see him and discuss a grievance.''

"What about you? What do you do?" she asked.

Mazin leaned back in his chair. "I am in the government. I coordinate oil production."

She had no idea what that might involve. If he was in the government and knew the royal family then he had to be a pretty important man. "Is it all right that you're here with me now?" she asked. "I wouldn't want you to get in trouble for taking the day off."

"Do not worry yourself," he told her with a slow smile. "I have plenty of vacation days available to me."

They walked along the beach after lunch. Mazin couldn't remember the last time he'd simply gone for a walk by the sea. Although he could see the ocean from nearly every window in his house, the view had ceased to be beautiful. He doubt he even saw it anymore.

Yet with Phoebe, all was new. She laughed with delight as waves rolled close and lapped at her feet. She'd rolled up the legs of her slacks, exposing her slender ankles. He studied the naked skin, amazed that he felt aroused gazing at her. She was completely dressed except for her bare feet and he *wanted* her.

Twenty-three, he reminded himself. She was only twenty-three. No younger than he had suspected, but younger than he had hoped.

"Is there a coral reef?" Phoebe asked.

''Not on this side of the island, but on the north end. The area is more protected there. Do you dive?''

She wrinkled her nose. ''I'm assuming you mean skin diving. I've never done it. I don't know that I could. Just the thought of being trapped underwater makes me nervous.''

As she spoke, she pulled her braid over her shoulder so the length of blond hair lay against her chest. She unfastened the ribbon, then finger-combed her hair so it fluttered loose around her face.

Sunlight illuminated the side of her face, highlighting her perfect bone structure. If she were any other woman of his acquaintance, he would have assumed she was going for an effect, but with Phoebe, he wasn't so sure. While he still thought she might be playing a game with him, several hours in her company had made him stop wondering about the sincerity of her innocence. She blushed too easily for someone at home in the world. And if she was as inexperienced as he suspected, then she was in danger of being taken advantage of by someone....

Someone like himself, he thought grimly. Someone who could easily pluck the flower of her womanhood, savor its sweetness, then discard it.

He did not consider himself a bad person. Perhaps Phoebe had been sent into his life as a test of that theory. Perhaps he was taking this too seriously. He should simply enjoy her company for the day, return her to her hotel that afternoon and forget he'd ever met her. That would be the wisest course of action.

"The ocean is very different here," Phoebe said as they continued to walk along the beach. "I don't have a lot of experience, but I know the color of the water is different than it is in Florida. Of course, the color is often a reflection of how shallow the water is. Around the gulf coast there are places you can wade out forever. Is it deeper here around the island?"

"Three sides are deep. The north end of the island is quite shallow."

Phoebe sighed softly to herself. Why couldn't she talk about something more interesting? Here she was strolling along a beautiful beach next to a charming man and she babbled on about ocean depth. *Be brilliant,* she ordered herself. Unfortunately she didn't have a lot of experience in the brilliant department.

"Would you like to have a seat?" he asked when they reached a cluster of rocks sticking out of the white sand.

She nodded and followed him to a flat rock warm from the sun. She dumped her shoes and purse on the sand, then slid next to him, careful to make sure they didn't touch. A light breeze teased at her hair and made goose bumps break out on her wet feet.

"Tell me about your great-aunt," he said. "What was her life like here on the island?"

Phoebe drew one knee to her chest and wrapped her arms around her leg. "Her mother owned a beauty shop in town and Ayanna learned to be a hairdresser there. When she was eighteen she went to work in the Parrot Bay Inn. Apparently back then it was an international hot spot.''

Mazin grinned. ''I have heard many stories about 'the old days,' as my father would call them. When people flew in from all over the world to spend a week or two in the Lucia-Serrat sun.''

''Ayanna said the same thing. She was young and beautiful, and she wanted a great romantic adventure.''

''Did she find it?''

Phoebe hesitated. ''Well, sort of. There were several men who wanted to marry her. She became engaged to one or two, always breaking it off. One of the men insisted she keep the ring. It was a lovely ruby ring. She wore it often.'' She smiled at the memory.

''If she broke the engagements, then they weren't romantic adventures,'' he said.

''You're right. I know the great love of her life was the crown prince. Apparently they were in love with each other, even though he was married. Eventually people found out and there was a great scandal. In the end, Ayanna had to leave.''

Mazin gazed out toward the ocean. ''I remember hearing something about that. Despite being such an old man, I was not alive then.''

''You're not so very old.''

He nodded regally. ''I'm pleased you think so.''

She wasn't sure if he was teasing or not. ''I don't think Ayanna ever heard from the prince again. She never admitted anything to me, but I have always suspected that in her heart of hearts she thought he would come find her. So her romance has an unhappy ending.''

''She lived in your country for many years. Didn't she marry?''

Phoebe shook her head. ''There were always men who wanted her, right up until she died. But although she enjoyed their company, she never loved any of them.''

''Did they love her?''

''Absolutely. She was wonderful. Charming, intelligent, funny and so lovely in every respect.''

He turned toward her, then placed his index finger under her chin. ''I would imagine you look much like her.''

Phoebe's eyes widened in surprise. ''Not at all. Ayanna was a great beauty. I don't look anything like her.''

How could he pretend to think she could even compare to Ayanna?

''You have a lovely face,'' he murmured, more to himself than her. ''Your eyes are the color of the sea on a cloudless day, your skin is as soft as silk.''

Phoebe felt heat flaring on her cheeks. Telling herself he wasn't really complimenting her didn't stop her from being embarrassed. She felt like some hick straight off the farm, with hay in her hair.

She pulled back slightly so that he wasn't touching her. ''Yes, well, you're very kind, but it's hard to ignore facts. I'm too tall and too skinny. Half the time I think I look like a boy more than a grown woman. It's fairly disheartening.''

Mazin gazed at her. His dark eyes seemed able to see into her soul. ''I would never mistake you for a boy.''

She couldn't look away. Her skin prickled as if she'd been in the sun too long. Maybe she had. Or maybe it was the island itself, weaving a magic spell around her.

''Men don't find me attractive,'' she said bluntly, because she couldn't think of anything else to say. ''Or interesting.''

''Not all men.''

Was it her imagination, or had he just moved a little closer? And was it suddenly really hot?

''Some men find you very attractive.''

She would have sworn he didn't actually say that last sentence, because his lips were too close to hers to be speaking. But she couldn't ask, because she was in shock. Tremendous shock. She even stopped breathing, because at that moment he kissed her.

Phoebe didn't know what to think or do. One minute she'd been sitting on a rock by the ocean trying not to babble, and the next a very handsome, very sophisticated older man was kissing her. On the lips. Which, she supposed, was where most people kissed. Just not her. Not ever. In fact—

*Stop thinking!*

Her mind obeyed, going blank. It was only then

that she realized his mouth was still on hers, which meant they were kissing. Which left her in the awkward position of having no clue as to what was expected of her.

The contact teased, making her want to lean into him. She liked the feel of his lips against hers and the way he placed one hand on her shoulder. She felt the heat of his fingers and the way his breath brushed across her cheek. She could see the dark fan of his lashes and the hint of stubble on his cheek. He smelled like sunshine, only more masculine.

Every part of her felt extrasensitive and her mouth trembled slightly.

He broke the kiss and opened his eyes, making her think perhaps hers should have been closed.

"You did not want me to do that," he said quietly.

She blinked several times. Not want her first kiss? Was he crazy? "No, it was great."

"But you didn't respond."

Humiliation washed over her. Phoebe slid off the rock onto the sand, then reached for her shoes. Before she could grab them, Mazin was at her side. He took her hands in his and somehow compelled her to look at him.

"What aren't you telling me?" he asked.

"Nothing." Everything, she thought.

"Phoebe."

He spoke in a warning tone that made her toes curl into the sand. She swallowed, then blurted the truth out all at once, or at least as much of it as she was willing to confess.

"I don't have a lot of experience with men. I never dated in high school, because I didn't fit in. Then Ayanna got sick and I spent the four years nursing her. That didn't leave time for a social life—not that I wanted one. The past six months I've been sad. So I'm not really good at the whole kissing thing."

She stopped talking and hoped he would buy her explanation without figuring out that no man had ever kissed her before.

She waited for him to say something. And waited. A smile teased at the corners of his mouth. His dark expression softened slightly. Then he cupped her face in his large, strong hands.

"I see," he murmured before once again touching his lips to hers.

It should have been the same kiss she'd just experienced. Weren't they all the same? But somehow this felt different. More intense. Her eyes fluttered closed before she realized what had happened. Oddly, the darkness comforted her. Her brain shut down as well, which was nice because in the quiet she could actually feel the contact of skin on skin.

He kissed her gently, yet with a hint of fire that left her breathless. Somehow she found the courage to kiss him back. Tiny electric tingles raced up and down her arms and legs, making her shiver. Mazin moved closer, until they were practically touching. He swept his thumbs across her cheeks, which made her

want to part her lips. When she did, she felt the light
brush of his tongue against hers.

The contact was as delightful as it was unexpected.
The tingles in her arms and legs turned into ripples
and she found it difficult to stand. She had to hold on
to him, so she rested her hands lightly on his shoulders. They were kissing. Really kissing.

He stroked her lightly, circling her, exciting her.
After a minute or so, she found the courage to do the
same to him. Every aspect of the experience was
amazing.

Of course, she'd read about this in books and seen
passionate kissing in the movies, but she'd never experienced it herself. It was glorious. No wonder teen-
agers were willing to do it for hours. She found herself wanting to do the same.

She liked everything about it—the way he tasted,
the scent of him, the heat flaring between them. Her
body felt light, as if she could float away. When he
released her face and wrapped his arms around her,
pulling her close, she knew there was nowhere else
on earth she wanted to be.

Their bodies touched. From shoulder to knee, they
pressed together. She'd never been so close to a man,
and was stunned to find every part of him was mus-
cled and hard. She felt positively delicate by com-
parison.

At last he drew back and rested his forehead
against hers.

"That was a surprise," he said, his voice low and husky.

"Did I do it wrong?" she asked before she could stop herself.

He laughed. "No, my dove. You kissed exactly right. Perhaps too right."

Their breath mingled. Phoebe felt all squishy inside. She wanted to stay close to him forever, kissing until the world ended.

Instead of reading her mind, Mazin straightened, then glanced at his watch.

"Unfortunately, duty calls," he said, then put his arm around her. "Come. I will see you back to your hotel."

She wanted to protest, but he'd already given her so much. In a single day she'd experienced more than she could ever have imagined.

"You've been very kind," she said, savoring the weight of his arm around her waist. He waited while she picked up her purse and shoes, then drew her close again.

"The pleasure was mine."

*Oh, please let him want to see me again.*

They walked to the car in silence. Once there, Mazin held open the passenger door.

Phoebe told herself not to be disappointed. One day was enough. She could survive on these memories for a long time. But before she slid into the car, he caught her hand and brought it to his lips.

"Tomorrow?" he asked in a whisper.

"Yes," she breathed in relief. "Tomorrow."

# Chapter 4

Phoebe stepped carefully along the stone path through the center of the botanical garden. A light rain had fallen early that morning, leaving all the plants clean and sweet smelling. Overhead tall trees blocked out most of the heat from the midday sun. It was a pretty darned perfect moment.

"There are legends about ancient pirates coming to the island," Mazin was saying. "Archaeologists haven't found any evidence of raiders on the island, but the stories persist." He smiled. "Children are warned that if they don't behave, they'll be taken from their beds in the middle of the night."

Phoebe laughed. "That should scare them into doing what they're supposed to."

"I'm not sure they actually believe in the ancient pirates."

"Did you?"

He hesitated, then grinned. "Perhaps when I was very small."

She tried to imagine him as a little boy and could not. She glanced at his strong profile, wondering if his features had ever looked childish and soft. Her gaze lingered on his mouth. Had he really kissed her yesterday? It seemed more like a dream than something that had actually happened.

The hem of her dress brushed against a bush growing out onto the path. Drops of water trickled onto her bare leg. She tugged on her short-sleeved jacket and knew that, dream or not, she had been foolish to put on a dress that morning. Slacks would have been more sensible.

Only, she hadn't been feeling very sensible. She'd wanted to look special for Mazin—pretty. As she didn't wear makeup or know how to do anything fancy with her hair, a dress had been her only option. Now that she was with him, she hoped he didn't realize she'd gone to any effort. Yesterday he had said kind things about her appearance, but she wasn't sure she believed the compliments. Of course she'd had plenty of time to relive them last night, when she'd barely slept at all.

"Are there other stories about the island?" she asked.

"Several. Legend has it that when there is a lunar eclipse visible from Lucia-Serrat, there is magic in

the air. Mysterious creatures are said to appear, and
animals can talk.''

''Really?''

He shrugged. ''I have no personal experience with
talking animals.''

A branch stretched across part of the path. Mazin
took her arm and led her around the obstruction.

His fingers were warm against her bare skin. Some
time before dawn it had crossed her mind that he
might be trying to seduce her. As she had no experience with the process, she couldn't be sure. If he
was, should she mind? Phoebe couldn't decide.

Her plan had always been to go to college and become a nurse. She knew little of love and less of
marriage. For years she'd had the feeling both were
going to pass her by—hence her education-career
plan. She wanted to be prepared to take care of herself.

But an affair was not marriage. She was on the
island for only a few weeks. If Mazin offered to teach
her the mysteries between a man and a woman, why
on earth would she say no?

They turned left at the next opportunity. Tall bam-
boo shared space with different kinds of bananas.
Some were small, some large. Many were unfamiliar.

''I've never seen anything like this,'' she said as
they paused next to a cluster of red bananas.

''Florida is tropical,'' he reminded her.

''I know, but where I live it's more suburban.
There are some exotic plants, but nothing like this.''

"You moved there when you were young, I believe?"

She hesitated. "Yes."

"You do not have to speak of your past if you do not wish to."

"I appreciate that. I don't have anything to hide." They began walking again. Phoebe folded her arms over her chest. She didn't mind talking about her life—she just didn't want him to think she was some backwater hick.

"I was born in Colorado. I never knew my father, and my mother didn't speak of him. Her parents died before I was born. She did…" Phoebe hesitated, her gaze firmly fixed on the ground. "She didn't like people very much. We lived in a small cabin in the middle of the woods. There weren't any other people around and we never had contact with the outside world. There was no electricity or indoor plumbing. We got all of our water from a well."

She cast a quick glance at Mazin. He seemed interested. "I did not know there were parts of your country without such amenities."

"There are some. My mother taught me to read, but didn't discuss much of the outside world with me. We were happy, I guess. I know she cared about me, but I was often lonely. One day when I was eight, we were out collecting berries. There was a lot of water from the spring snow runoff higher in the mountain. She slipped on some wet leaves, fell and hit her head. I found out later that she died instantly, but at the time I didn't know why she wouldn't wake up. After a few hours, I knew I had to go get help, even though she had always forbidden me to have anything to do with other people. There was a town about ten miles away. I'd stumbled across it a couple of times when I'd been out exploring.''

Mazin stopped walking and grabbed her by her upper arms. "You had never been into the town before?"

She shook her head.

"You must have been terrified."

"I was more scared that there was something wrong with my mother, or that she was going to be mad when she woke up." She sighed, remembering how she'd been trying so hard not to cry as she explained what had happened to several strangers before one of them finally took her to the sheriff's office.

"They went and got her," she said. Mazin released her arms and she started walking. It seemed easier to keep moving as she talked. "Then they told me she was dead. I didn't know what it meant for a long time."

"Where did you go?"

"Into a temporary foster home until they could locate a relative. It took about six months, because I didn't know anything about my family. They had to go through all of her personal effects to get leads. In the meantime I had to adjust to a life that everyone else took for granted. It was hard."

Those three words couldn't possibly explain what

it had been like, Phoebe thought. She still remembered her shock the first time she'd seen an indoor bathroom. The toilet had stunned her, while the idea of *hot* running water on demand had been a taste of heaven.

"I started school, of course," she said.

"You must have had difficulties."

"Just a couple. I knew how to read, but I'd had no education. Math was a mystery to me. I knew my numbers, but nothing else. Plus I'd missed all the socialization that most children undergo. I didn't know how to make friends, and I'd never seen a television, let alone a movie."

"Your mother had no right to do that to you."

She glanced at him, surprised by the fierceness in his voice. "She did what she thought was best. Sometimes I think I understand, other times I'm angry."

They stepped into the sun and Phoebe was grateful for the warmth.

They walked in silence for several minutes. There were things about her past that she'd never admitted to anyone, not even Ayanna. Her aunt had been so kind and supportive from the first that she hadn't wanted to trouble her.

"I didn't make friends easily," Phoebe whispered. "I didn't know how. The other children knew I was different and they stayed away from me. I was grateful when they found my aunt, not only to have a home, but to get away from the loneliness."

Mazin led her to a bench on the side of the path.

She settled in a corner, her hands clasped tightly together, the memories growing larger in her mind.

"Ayanna drove out to get me. Later she told me it was because she thought the car trip would give us time to get to know each other." She smiled sadly. "Her plan worked. By the time we reached Florida, I was comfortable with her. And I did a little better making friends. I'd learned from previous mistakes. Unfortunately, I had more trouble in school. For a while the teachers were convinced I was retarded. I couldn't even score well on the IQ tests because I didn't have the frame of reference to answer the questions."

"Yet you were successful."

She nodded. "It took a long time. Ayanna took me to the library every week and helped me pick out different books so that I could learn about things. It's the little things, like knowing that the word *pipe* has two meanings."

She suddenly realized how long she'd been talking, and groaned. "I'm sorry. I don't even remember what you asked me. I know you couldn't have wanted this long answer."

"I'm happy to hear about your past," Mazin told her, lightly touching the back of her hand. "I am impressed by your ability to overcome a disadvantage."

She supposed his answer should have pleased her, but it didn't. She wanted him to see her as someone he could find exciting, not as an example of a job well done. She wanted him to take her in his arms again and kiss her thoroughly.

With a fierceness that both shocked and frightened her, she found herself wishing that he *did* want to seduce her.

But instead of kissing her or even holding her close, he rose.

Reluctantly she got to her feet.

They continued to walk through the garden. Mazin was a most attentive host, pointing out plants of interest, inquiring about her state of well-being in the hot morning. As the sun rose in the sky, her spirits plummeted. She shouldn't have told him about her strange upbringing. She shouldn't have spilled her secrets. How could he think of her as anything but odd?

"You have grown silent," Mazin said when he realized Phoebe had stopped talking.

She shrugged.

He took in the slump of her shoulders and the way her fingers endlessly pleated her skirt. "Why are you sad?"

"I'm not. I just feel…" She pressed her lips together. "I don't want you to think I'm stupid."

"Why would I think that?"

"Because of what I told you."

She had told him about her past. From his perspective, the information had only made her more dangerous. Yesterday she had been a pretty woman who attracted him sexually. Their kiss had shown him the possibilities and the accompanying arousal had

disturbed his sleep. Today he knew that she was more
than an appealing body. He knew that she had a
strong spirit and that she had succeeded against impossible odds. Why would that make him think she
was stupid?

Women were complex creatures.

"Put it from your mind, my dove," he told her,
taking her hand in his. "I admire your ability to overcome your past. Come, I will show your our English
rose garden. Some of the rosebushes are very ancient,
and still annoyed to find themselves so far from
home."

The next morning Phoebe had almost convinced
herself that Mazin meant what he said—that he admired her for her past. However, she couldn't quite
embrace the concept, mostly because he hadn't kissed
her goodbye. He'd kissed her on the first day, but not
on the second. Didn't that mean they were moving in
the wrong direction?

She stood in front of the bathroom mirror and
pulled her hair back into a ponytail. As the dress
hadn't created any magic the day before, she was
back in slacks and a T-shirt. Maybe now he would
want to kiss her.

She finished with her hair and dropped her hands
to her side. After only two days in the company of a
handsome man, her brain was spinning. It was probably for the best that there hadn't been any kissing.

Except she'd really enjoyed how she'd felt in his arms.

"At least I'm having an adventure, Ayanna," she said as she smoothed sunscreen on her arms. "That should make you happy."

She was still smiling at the thought of her aunt's pleasure when the phone rang. Phoebe turned to look at it, her stomach clenching. There was only one person who would be calling her, and she already knew the reason.

"Hello?"

"Phoebe, this is Mazin. Something has come up and I will not be able to join you today."

She was sure he said more, that he kept talking, but she couldn't hear anything. She sank onto the bed and closed her eyes.

He wasn't coming. He was bored with her. He thought she was a child, or maybe he'd been lying when he'd said he appreciated her past. It doesn't matter, she told herself, squeezing in the pain. This trip wasn't about him—it never had been. How could she have forgotten?

"I appreciate you letting me know," she said brightly, interrupting him. "I'll let you get back to your day and I must begin mine. There is so much to see on this beautiful island. Thank you, Mazin. Good-bye."

Then she hung up before she did something stupid like cry.

It took her fifteen minutes to fight back tears and

another ten to figure out what she was going to do. Her aunt had specifically left her the money to visit Lucia-Serrat. Phoebe couldn't repay her by wasting time sulking. She read Ayanna's list and then studied the guidebook. The church of St. Mary was within walking distance. Next to that was a dog park. If the beauty of the architecture and stained glass didn't ease the disappointment in her heart, then the antics of the dogs would make her laugh.

That decided, Phoebe headed out on her own. She found the church, a stunning structure with high arches and cool interiors. She admired the carvings and let the silence and peace ease her pain.

She'd known Mazin only a little over two days, she told herself as she sat in a rear pew. He had been more than kind. It was wrong and foolish of her to expect more of him. As for the kiss and her fantasies that he might want to seduce her, well, at least she *had* been kissed. The next time, with the next man, she would do better. Eventually she would figure out how to be normal.

She left the church and walked to the dog park. As she'd hoped, there were dozens of dogs playing, running and barking. She laughed over the antics of several small dalmatian puppies and helped an older woman put her Irish setter in the back of her car.

By the time she stopped for lunch her spirits had risen to the point where she could chat with the waitress about the menu and not think about Mazin.

While waiting for her entrée, she made friends with

the older English couple at the next table, and they recommended she try the boat tour that went around the island. The trip took all day and offered impressive views of Lucia-Serrat. As they were all staying at the Parrot Bay Inn, they walked back together and Phoebe stopped at the concierge desk to pick up a brochure on the boat trip. Then she headed up to her room, pleasantly tired and pleased that she'd gotten through the day without thinking of Mazin more than two or three dozen times.

Tomorrow she would do better, she promised herself. By next week, she would barely remember his name.

But when she entered her room, the first thing she noticed was a new, larger spray of flowers. Her fingers trembled as she opened the card.

"Something lovely for my beautiful dove. I'm sorry I could not be with you today. I will be thinking of you. Mazin."

Her throat tightened and her eyes burned as she read the card. She didn't have to compare the handwriting with that on the first card she'd received— she knew they were the same. The fact that he had just been trying to be nice didn't lessen her pain. Perhaps she was being foolish and acting like a child, but she missed him.

The phone rang, interrupting her thoughts. Phoebe cleared her throat, then picked up the receiver.

"Hello?"

"Here I had imagined you spending the day pining

for me when in truth you were out having a good
time.''

Her heart jumped into her throat. She could barely
breathe. ''Mazin?''

''Of course. What other man would call you?''

Despite her loneliness, she couldn't help smiling.
''Maybe there are dozens.''

''I wouldn't be surprised.'' He sighed. ''Aren't you
going to ask me how I knew you weren't alone in
your room, pining for me?''

''How did you know?''

''I've been calling and you have not been there.''

Her heart returned to her chest and began to flutter,
even though she knew she was a fool. ''I went to the
church and the dog park. Then I had lunch. A lovely
couple told me about the boat tour around the island.
I thought I might do that tomorrow.''

''I see.''

She plowed ahead. ''You've been more than kind,
but I know you have your own life and your own
responsibilities.''

''What if I wish to see you? Are you telling me
no?''

She clutched the receiver so hard, her fingers hurt.
Tears pooled in her eyes. ''I don't understand.''

''Nor do I.''

She wiped away her tears. ''Th-thank you for the
flowers.''

''You are welcome. I am sorry about today.'' He

sighed. "Phoebe, if you would rather not spend time with me, I will abide by your wishes."

Tears flowed faster. The odd thing was she couldn't say exactly *why* she was crying. "It's not that."

"Why is your voice shaking?"

"It's n-not."

"You're crying."

"Maybe."

"Why?"

"I don't know."

"Would it help if I said I was disappointed, as well? That I would rather be with you than reading boring reports and spending my day in endless meetings?"

"Yes, that would help a lot."

"Then know that it is true. Tell me you'll see me tomorrow."

A sensible woman would refuse, she thought, knowing Mazin would not only distract her from her plans for her future, but that he would also likely break her heart.

"I'll see you tomorrow."

"Good. I will see you then."

She nodded. "Goodbye, Mazin."

"Goodbye, my dove. Until tomorrow. I promise to make the day special."

He hung up. She carefully replaced the phone, knowing that he didn't have to try to make the day special. Just by showing up he would brighten her world.

# Chapter 5

"Where are we going?" Phoebe asked for the third time since Mazin had picked her up that morning. They'd already toured the marketplace, after which he had promised a surprise.

"You will see when we arrive," he said with a smile. "Be patient, my dove."

"You're driving me crazy," she told him. "I think you're doing it on purpose."

"Perhaps."

She tried to work up a case of righteous indignation, but it was not possible. Not with the sun shining in the sky and the beauty of Lucia-Serrat all around them. Not with Mazin sitting next to her in his car, spending yet another day with her.

She had known him little more than two weeks.

They had spent a part of nearly every day together, although not any evenings. So far they'd worked their way through a good portion of Ayanna's list. Phoebe had seen much of the island, including a view from the ocean on the tour boat.

"Is it a big place, or a small place?" she asked.

"A big place."

"But it is not on my list."

"No."

She sighed. "Did my aunt visit there?"

"I would think so."

They drove toward the north end of the island, heading inland. Gradually the road began to rise. Phoebe tried to picture the map of the island in her mind. What was in this direction? Then she reminded herself it didn't really matter. She had memories stored up for her return home. When she was deep in her studies, she would remind herself of her time on Lucia-Serrat, when a handsome man had made her feel special.

She glanced at him out of the corner of her eye. He was concentrating on his driving and did not notice her attention. Although he was unfailingly polite, he had yet to kiss her again. She wasn't sure why, and her lack of experience with men kept her from speculating. She thought it might have something to do with the fact that she *was* inexperienced, but couldn't confirm the information. Asking was out of the question.

They rounded a corner. Up ahead, through a grove of trees, a tall house reached up toward the sky. She squinted. Actually it was more of a castle than a house, or maybe a palace.

A palace?

Mazin inclined his head. "The official residence of the prince. He has a private home, but that is not open to the public. Although this is not on your Ayanna's list, I thought you might enjoy strolling through the grounds and exploring the public rooms."

She turned to him and smiled with delight. "I would love to see it. Thank you for thinking of this, Mazin. My aunt came here often to attend the famous parties. She danced with the prince in the grand ballroom."

"Then we will make sure we see that part of the castle."

They drove around to a small parking lot close to the building. Phoebe glanced at the larger public lot they had passed on their way in.

"You forget I have a position of some importance in the government," he said, reading her mind as he opened his car door. "Parking here is one of the perks."

He climbed out of the car, then came around to her side and opened the door. Phoebe appreciated the polite gesture. Sometimes she even let herself fantasize that he was being more than polite, that his actions had significance. Then she remembered she was a nobody from Florida and that he was a successful, older man simply being kind. Besides, she had her life already planned. Okay, maybe her plan wasn't as exciting as her imaginings about Mazin, but it was far more real.

"This way," he said, taking her hand in his and heading for the palace. "The original structure was built at the time of the spice trade."

"You told me that the crown prince is always a relative of the king of Bahania. He was probably used to really nice houses."

Mazin flashed her a grin. "Exactly. Originally the prince lived in the palace, but as you can see, while it is a beautiful palace, it is not especially large. Quarters were cramped with the prince's family, his children and their children, various officials, servants, visiting dignitaries. So in the late 1800s the prince had a private residence constructed."

Mazin paused on the tree-lined path and pointed. "You can see a bit of it through there."

Phoebe tilted her head. She caught a glimpse of a corner of a building and several windows. "It looks nearly as big as the palace."

"Apparently the building project grew a little."

She returned her attention to the graceful stone palace in front of them. "So official business occurs here? At least the prince doesn't have much of a commute."

"I'm sure he appreciates that."

They crossed the ground around to the front of the palace. Phoebe still felt a little uneasy about trespassing, but as Mazin wasn't worried, she did her best to enjoy the moment. He was a knowledgeable host, explaining the different styles of architecture and telling her amusing stories from the past.

"Now we will go inside," he said. "Our first stop will be the ballroom."

They headed for the main gates overlooking the ocean. As they crossed the open drawbridge, a distant call caught Phoebe's attention. She looked toward the sound. A small boy raced toward them, down the length of the drawbridge. Dark hair flopped in his face, while his short, sturdy legs pumped furiously.

"Papa, Papa, wait for me!"

Phoebe didn't remember stopping, but suddenly she wasn't moving. She stared at the boy, then slowly turned her attention to Mazin. Her host watched the child with a combination of affection and exasperation.

"My son," he said unnecessarily.

Phoebe was saved from speaking by the arrival of the boy. He flew at his father. Mazin caught him easily, pulling him close into an embrace that was both loving and comfortable. They obviously did this a lot.

A tightness in her chest told her that she'd stopped breathing. Phoebe gasped once, then wondered if she looked as shocked as she felt. She knew Mazin was older. Of course he would have lived a full life, and it made sense that his life might include children. But intellectualizing about a possibility and actually meeting a child were two very different things.

Mazin shifted his son so that the boy sat on his left forearm. One small arm encircled his neck. They both turned to her.

"This is my son, Dabir. Dabir, this is Miss Carson."

"Hello," the boy said, regarding her with friendly curiosity.

"Hi." Phoebe wasn't sure if she was expected to shake hands.

He appeared to be five or six, with thick dark hair and eyes just like his father. She had been unable to picture Mazin as a child, but now, looking at Dabir, she saw the possibilities.

Mazin settled his free hand at Dabir's waist. "So tell us what you're doing here at the castle. Don't you have lessons today?"

"I learned all my numbers and got every question right, so I got a reward." He grinned at Phoebe. "I told Nana I wanted to see the swords, so she brought me here. Have you seen them? They're long and scary."

He practically glowed as he spoke. Obviously viewing the swords was a favorite treat.

Phoebe tried to answer, but her lips didn't seem to be working. Mazin spoke for her.

"We were just about to walk into the castle. We haven't seen anything yet. Miss Carson is visiting Lucia-Serrat for the first time."

"Do you like it?" Dabir asked.

"Um, yes. It's lovely."

The boy beamed. "I'm six. I have three older brothers. They're all much bigger than me, but I'm the favorite."

Mazin set the boy on the ground and ruffled his hair. "You are not the favorite, Dabir. I love all my sons equally."

Dabir didn't seem the least bit upset by the announcement. He giggled and leaned against his father, while studying her.

"Do you have any children?" he asked.

"No. I'm not married."

Dabir's eyes widened. "Do you like children?"

Phoebe hadn't thought the situation could get more uncomfortable, yet it just had. "I, ah, like them very much."

"Enough," Mazin said, his voice a low growl. "Go find Nana."

Dabir hesitated, as if he would disobey, then he waved once and raced back into the castle. Phoebe watched him go. Children. Mazin had children. Four of them. All boys.

"He's very charming," she forced herself to say when they were alone.

Mazin turned toward her and cupped her face. "I could read your mind. You must never try to play poker, my dove. Your thoughts are clearly visible to anyone who takes the time to look."

There was a humiliating thought. She sighed. "You have lived a very full life," she said. "Of course you would have children."

"Children, but no wife."

Relief filled her. She hadn't actually allowed herself to think the question, but she was happy to hear the answer.

"Come," he said, taking her hand in his. "I will show you the ballroom where your Ayanna danced. As we walk, I will tell you all about my sordid past."

"Is it so very bad?"

"I'm not sure. Your standards will be higher than most. You will have to tell me."

They walked into the castle. She tried to catch a glimpse of Dabir and his Nana, but they seemed to have disappeared.

"Some of the tapestries date back to the twelfth century," he said, motioning to the delicate wall hangings.

She dutifully raised her gaze to study them. "They're very nice."

Mazin sighed, then pulled her toward a bench by the stone wall. "Perhaps we should deal with first things first, as you Americans like to say."

He sat on the bench and pulled her next to him. She had the brief thought that actually sitting on furniture in the royal castle might be punishable by imprisonment, or worse, but then Mazin took her hands in his and she couldn't think at all.

"I am a widower," he told her, staring into her eyes. "My wife died giving birth to Dabir. We have three boys. And I have another son from a brief liaison when I was a young man."

That last bit of news nearly sent her over the edge, but all she said was "Oh."

Four sons. It seemed like a large number of children for one man. No wonder he hadn't been spending his evenings with her; he had a family waiting at home. If they were all as charming as Dabir, he must hate being away from them.

"I've been keeping you from them," she said

softly. "I've told you that you don't have to keep me company."

"I choose to be here."

She wanted to ask why, but didn't have the courage. "You must have help with them. Dabir mentioned Nana."

He smiled. "Yes. She is a governess of sorts for my youngest. The two middle boys are in a private boarding school. My oldest is at university in England."

She tried not to show her shock. "How old is he?"

"Nearly twenty. I am much older than you, Phoebe. Did you forget?"

"No, it's just…" She did the math. He'd had a child when he'd been seventeen? She was twenty-three and had been kissed only once. Could they be more different?

"I know you say you choose to be here," she said, "but you have a family and work obligations. I must be a distraction. Please don't be concerned. I'm very capable of entertaining myself. How could I not enjoy my time on this beautiful island?"

"Ah, but if you remain alone, you will never be able to visit Lucia's Point."

She ducked her head as heat flared on her cheeks. Lucia's Point—the place for lovers. It seemed unlikely that she would be visiting that particular spot on this trip.

A horrifying thought occurred to her. She tried to push it away, but it refused to budge. Then she found herself actually voicing it aloud as she risked looking at him.

"You have four sons, Mazin. Do you see me as the daughter you never had?"

He released her hands at once. She didn't know what that meant, but she was aware of his dark eyes brightening with many emotions. None of them seemed paternal.

"Do you see me as the father you never had?"

Her blush deepened. "No," she whispered. "I never thought of that."

"I do not think of you as a child, especially not my own. On the contrary. I see you very much as a woman."

"Do you? I want to believe you, but I've lived such a small life."

"It is the quality of one's life that matters."

"Easy to say when you had your first affair at seventeen," she blurted before she could stop herself. She pressed her fingers to her mouth, horrified, but Mazin only laughed.

"An interesting point. Come. We will walk to the ballroom. When we are there, I will tell you all about my affair with the ever-beautiful Carnie."

"She was an actress," Mazin said ten minutes later as they strolled through a vast open area.

Tall, slender windows let in light. Dozens of candelabras hung from an arched ceiling. There was a stage in one corner, probably for an orchestra, and enough space to hold a football game.

Phoebe tried to imagine the room filled with people dressed in their finest, dancing the night away, but she was still caught up in his description of his first mistress as "ever beautiful."

"*Was* she very lovely?" she asked before she could stop herself.

"Yes. Her face and body were perfection. However, she had a cold heart. I learned very quickly that I was more interested in a woman's inner beauty than her outside perfection."

His statement made her feel better. Phoebe knew that in a competition of straight looks, she wouldn't have a chance, but she thought her heart would stand up all right.

"We met when the film company came here to shoot part of a movie. She was an older woman— nearly twenty-two. I was very impressed with myself at the time and determined to have her."

She didn't doubt he'd achieved his goal. "What happened when you found out she was pregnant?"

He took her hand in his. The pressure of his palm against her, the feel of their fingers laced together nearly distracted her from his words.

"She was upset. I don't know if she'd hoped for marriage, but it was out of the question. My father…" He hesitated. "The family did not approve. We had money, so an offer was made. She accepted."

Phoebe stared at him. "Didn't you love her?"

"Perhaps for the first few weeks, but it faded. When I found out about the child, I wanted my son, but I didn't think Carnie and I had much chance at happiness. She stayed long enough to have the baby, then left.''

''I could never do that,'' Phoebe said, completely shocked by Carnie's behavior. ''I would never give up my child. I don't care how much money was involved.''

Mazin shrugged. ''I don't think my father gave her much choice.''

''That wouldn't matter. I would stand up against anyone. I'd go into hiding.''

''Carnie preferred the cash.''

Mazin heard the harshness in his voice. Most of the time he was at peace with his former lover, but occasionally he despised her for what she had done, even though it had made his life simpler.

''Is she still alive?''

''Yes, but she rarely sees her son. It is better that way.''

He watched the play of emotions across Phoebe's face. She was so easy to read. She was outraged by Carnie's decision, yet it went against her nature to judge anyone negatively. Her wide mouth trembled slightly at the corners and her delicate brows drew together as she tried to reconcile harsh facts with her gentle nature.

She was a good person. He couldn't say that very often, not with certainty. She wanted nothing from him, save his company. Their time was a balm and he found himself in need of the healing only she could provide. Being with her made him quiet and content. Two very rare commodities in his life.

She had been startled by Dabir's sudden appearance. Mazin had been, as well, but for different reasons. He had seen something as he'd watched her. Over the past six years he had become an expert at judging a woman's reaction to his children. Some pretended to like them because they wanted to be his wife. Some genuinely enjoyed the company of children. He put Phoebe in the latter category.

He liked her. Mazin couldn't remember the last time he had simply liked a woman. He also wanted her. The combination caused more than a little discomfort. Because he cared about her, he refused to push her into his bed, which was exactly where he wanted her to be. Holding back was not his style, yet this time it felt right.

She was different from anyone he'd ever known. He suspected she would say the same about him.

"Phoebe, you must know I'm a rich man," he said.

She bit her bottom lip. "I sort of figured that out."

"Does that bother you?"

"A little."

She glanced at him. Her long blond hair fell down her back. He wanted to capture it in his hands and feel the warm silk of the honeyed strands. He wanted many things.

"I don't understand why you spend time with me," she said in a rush. "I like being with *you,* but I worry that you're bored."

He smiled. "Never. Do you remember yesterday when we went to see the meerkats?"

"Yes?"

"You fed them their lunch of fruits and vegetables. You were patient, feeding each in its turn, never tired."

She sighed. "They were wonderful. So cute and funny. I could watch them for hours. I love how they stand guard, watching out for each other."

"You told me you'd seen a show about African meerkats and how one was burned in a fire."

She stopped walking. He moved to stand in front of her. As they had the previous day, her eyes filled up with tears.

"It tried to stand guard, but couldn't," she whispered. "They all huddled around it. Then a couple of days later, it left the group and went off to die."

A single tear rolled down her cheek. Mazin touched it with his finger. "Tears for a meerkat. What would you give to a child in need?"

"I don't understand the question."

"I know, but these tears are why I am not bored with you."

She sniffed. "You're making absolutely no sense."

He laughed. "You would find others to agree with you. So tell me, what do you want from your life?"

Her blue eyes widened slightly. "Me? Nothing special. I'd like children. Three or four, at least. And a house. But before any of that, I want to get my degree."

"In what?"

"Nursing. I like taking care of people."

He remembered her dying aunt. Yes, Phoebe would do well with the sick.

"I would like—" She shook her head. "Sorry.

This can't be interesting. My dreams are very small and ordinary. Like I said, a small life. I'm not sure there's all that much quality there.''

''On the contrary. You have much to recommend you.''

Then, against his better judgment, he pulled her close.

She came willingly into his arms, as he had known she would. Her body pressed against him, her arms wrapped around him. She raised her head in a silent offering, and he did not have the strength of will to deny her.

He touched his mouth to hers. This time she responded eagerly, kissing him back. He kept the contact light, because if he took what he really wanted, they would make love here in the public rooms of the castle. So he nipped at her lower lip and trailed kisses along her jaw. He slid his hands up and down her back, careful to avoid the tempting curves of her rear.

Her breathing accelerated as he licked the hollow of her throat. She wore a dress with a slightly scooped neck. The thrust of her small breasts called to him. It would be so easy to move lower. He could see the outline of her tight nipples straining against the fabric of her clothing. Desire filled him with an intensity that made him ache.

Good sense won. He returned his attentions to her mouth. She parted in invitation. He might be able to resist her other temptations, but not that one. He had to taste her sweetness one more time.

He plunged into her. She accepted his conquest and

began an assault of her own. Just once, he thought hazily, and slipped his hand onto the curve of her hip. She responded by drawing closer, pressing her breasts against his chest and breathing his name.

Mazin swore. Phoebe was very much an innocent, and she didn't know what she was offering.

He wanted her and he couldn't have her. Not only because she was a virgin, but because he hadn't told her the truth about everything. At first he'd withheld the information because it had amused him. Now he found he didn't want her to know.

He forced himself to pull back. They were both breathing heavily. Phoebe smiled at him.

''You've probably heard this a thousand times before,'' she said, ''but you're a really good kisser.''

He laughed. ''As are you.''

''If I am, it's because of you.''

The blush of arousal stained her cheeks; her lips were swollen. Her beauty touched him deep in his soul. He wanted to see her in diamonds and satin.

He wanted to see her in nothing at all.

''What are you thinking?'' she asked.

''That you are an unexpected delight in my life.''

Her blue eyes darkened with emotion that he didn't want to read. Slowly, tentatively she touched his mouth with her fingertip. Her breath caught in her throat.

''What do you want from me, Mazin?''

He found himself compelled to speak the truth. ''I don't know.''

# Chapter 6

Phoebe pulled a chair close to the balcony and stared out at the stars. The balmy night air brushed against her bare arms, making her tremble slightly, although she couldn't say why. It wasn't that she was cold or even fearful. She knew in her heart that nothing bad could happen while she was on the island.

Perhaps it was the memory of Mazin's kiss that made her unable to keep still. Something had happened that afternoon when he'd taken her in his arms. She'd seen something in his eyes, something that had made her think this might not just be a game to him. His inability to tell her what he wanted from her made her both happy and nervous. One of them had to know what was going on, and she didn't have a clue. Which left Mazin.

She pulled her knees to her chest and wrapped her arms around her legs. Her long white cotton nightgown fluttered in the breeze.

There had been a difference in his kiss today. An intensity that had shaken her to her core. Did he want her that way? Did he want to make love with her? Did she want to make love with him?

He was not the man she had fantasized about. In her mind, Mazin had no life, save that time he spent with her. Now she knew that he had been a husband. He was a father, with four sons. He had a life that didn't include her, and when she was gone, he would return to it as if she'd never been here at all.

Were all his sons like Dabir? She smiled at the memory of the bright, loving little boy. Spending time with him would be a joy.

Several years of baby-sitting had taught her to assess a child very quickly. Dabir would no doubt get into plenty of trouble, but he had a generous heart and a sense of fun. She bit her lower lip. One child would be easy, but four? Worse, Mazin's oldest was only a few years younger than she was. The thought made her shiver. Not that Mazin's children were going to be an issue, she reminded herself.

Phoebe stared up at the stars, but the night skies didn't hint at how long until Mazin grew tired of her, nor did they whisper his intent. Instead of meeting her during the day tomorrow, Mazin had arranged for them to spend the evening together. Somehow the change of time made her both excited and nervous.

No matter what, she told herself, she would never have regrets. Just as Ayanna had made her promise.

Moonlight sparkled on the ever-shifting ocean. Phoebe breathed in the scent of sea spray and nearby flowers. Whatever else might happen in her life, she would remember this night forever.

Mazin sat across from her, handsome as always. Tonight he wore a suit, making her glad she'd spent more than she should have for a pretty blouse in the hotel boutique. Her slim black skirt had seen better days, but it was serviceable enough. After nearly an hour of fussing with her hair, she'd managed to pin it up into a French twist. She felt almost sophisticated. Something she would need to counteract the effect of Mazin's attraction by moonlight.

''I feel a little guilty,'' she said as the waiter poured from the wine bottle.

''Why?'' Mazin asked when the waiter had left and they were alone. ''Have you done something you should not have done?''

''No.'' She smiled. ''But it's evening. You should be home with your family.''

''Ah. You are thinking of my children.''

Among other things, she thought, hoping he couldn't read her mind and know how many times she had relived their kisses.

''Dabir, especially,'' she murmured. ''Wouldn't you rather be home, tucking him in bed?''

Mazin dismissed her with a shake of his head. "He is six. Far too old to be tucked in bed by his father."

"He's practically a baby, not a teenager."

Mazin frowned. "I had not thought he would still need that sort of attention. He has Nana to take care of him."

"That's not the same as having you around."

"Are you trying to get rid of me?"

"Not at all. I just don't want you to take time away from them to be with me. I know if I had children, I would want to be with them always."

One corner of his mouth turned up. "What of your husband's needs for you? Would they not come first?"

"I think he'd have to learn to compromise."

Mazin's humor turned to surprise. "It is the children and the wife who must compromise." He shrugged. "Most of the time. I was married long enough to have learned that on rare occasions the man does not come first."

"I should think not." She leaned toward him. "Tell me about your sons."

"Why do I sense you are more interested in them than in me?"

"I'm not. It's just…" She hesitated, then decided there was no point in avoiding the truth. "I find the subject of your children very safe."

"Because I am unsafe?"

Rather than answer, she took a sip of her wine.

He chuckled and reached forward, capturing her

free hand in his. "I know you, my dove. I have learned to read you when you avoid my eyes and busy yourself with a task. You do not wish to respond to my question. Now my job is to learn why."

He studied her, his dark eyes unreadable. She wished she could know him as well as he seemed to know her.

"Why do you fear me?" he asked unexpectedly.

Phoebe was so surprised that she straightened, pulling her hand free of his. She clutched her fingers together on her lap.

"I'm not afraid." She bit her lower lip. "Well, not too afraid," she added, because she'd never been much of a liar. "It's just that you're different from anyone I've ever met. You're very charming, but also intimidating. I'm out of my element with you."

"Not so very far." He patted the table. "Put your hand here so that I may touch you."

He spoke matter-of-factly, but his words made her whole body shiver. She managed to slide her hand over to his, where he linked their fingers together. He felt strong and warm. He made her feel safe, which was odd because he was the reason she felt out of sorts in the first place.

"See?" he said. "We fit together well."

"I don't think that's true. I don't know why you spend so much time with me. I can't be anything like the other women in your life."

Now it was his turn to stiffen. He didn't pull his hand away, but ice crept into his gaze. "What other women?'' he asked curtly. ''What are you talking about?''

She sensed that she had insulted him. ''Mazin, I didn't mean anything specific. Just that I can see that you're a handsome, successful man. There must be dozens of women throwing themselves at you all the time. I have this picture of you having to step over them wherever you go.''

She wanted to say more, but her throat tightened at the thought of him being with anyone else, even though it probably happened all the time.

''Do not worry, my dove,'' he said softly. ''I have forgotten them all.''

For how long?

She only thought the question. There was no point in asking. After all, Mazin might tell her the truth, and that would hurt her.

''I can see you do not believe me,'' he said, releasing her fingers. ''To prove myself, I have brought you something.''

He snapped his fingers. Their waiter appeared, but instead of bringing menus, he carried a large flat box. Mazin took it from him and handed it to her.

''Do not say you can't accept until you have opened it. Because I know in my heart that once you see my offering, you won't be able to refuse it.''

''Then I should refuse it before I see it,'' she said.

''That is not allowed.''

Phoebe lightly touched the gold paper around the box. She tried to imagine what could be inside. Not jewelry. The box was far too big—at least eighteen inches by twelve. Not clothes—the box was too slender.

"You won't be able to guess," he told her. "Open it."

She slipped off the bow, then pulled the paper from the box. When she lifted the lid and drew back the tissue, her breath caught in her throat.

Mazin had given her a framed picture of Ayanna.

Phoebe recognized the familiar face immediately. Her great-aunt looked very young, perhaps only a year or two older than Phoebe was now. She stood alone, in front of a pillar. Behind her, open archways led to the ocean. She recognized the palace at once.

Ayanna wore a formal ball gown. Diamonds glittered from her ears, wrists and throat. With her hair pulled back and her posture so straight and regal, she looked as elegant as a princess.

"I've never seen this picture before," she breathed. "Where did you find it?"

"There are photographic archives. You had mentioned that your aunt was a favorite with the crown prince. I thought there might be pictures of her, and I was right. This one was taken at a formal party at the prince's private residence. The original remains in the archives, but they allowed me to make a copy."

She didn't know what to say. That he would have gone to all this trouble for her moved her beyond words. Still, she had to make an attempt to speak. "You're right. I can't refuse this gift. It means too much. I have a few pictures of Ayanna, but not nearly enough. Thank you for being so thoughtful and kind.''

''My only motive was to make you smile.''

She didn't care what his motive had been. There was no other present in the world that could have had so much meaning. Phoebe didn't know how to explain all the feelings welling up inside her. She wanted to go to Mazin and wrap her arms around him. She wanted to try to explain her gratitude, and she wanted him to kiss her until she couldn't think or speak or do anything but respond to him. Her eyes burned with unshed tears, her heart ached and there was a hollow place inside that she couldn't explain.

''I don't understand you,'' she said at last.

''Understanding isn't necessary.''

She wondered what was.

He sipped his wine. ''In two nights there is a celebration of the heritage of Lucia-Serrat,'' he said. ''While we are a tropical paradise, our roots are in the desert of Bahania. Along with a special meal, there will be entertainment. Dancers and music. Although this event is not on your Ayanna's list, I suspect you would enjoy yourself. If you are available that evening, I would be honored if you would accompany me.''

As if she had other plans. As if she would rather be with anyone but him. ''Thank you for asking me, Mazin. The honor of accompanying you is mine.''

He stared at her, his dark eyes seeing into her soul.

"It is probably for the best that you cannot read my mind," he murmured. "All that is between you and the death of your innocence is a thin thread of honor that even now threatens to unravel."

Once again he left her speechless. But before she could try to figure out if he really meant what he said—and deal with the sudden heat she felt in her belly—the waiter appeared with their menus. The mood was broken. Mazin made a great show of putting the picture safely back in the box. They discussed what they would have for dinner. His comment was never again mentioned.

But Phoebe didn't forget.

Two days later, a large box was delivered to her room. Phoebe knew instantly that it was from Mazin, but what could he be sending her? She unfastened the large bow and ribbon holding it in place, then lifted the cover.

Moving aside several layers of tissue revealed a dark blue evening gown that shimmered as she lifted it up to examine the style. Her breath caught in her throat. The silky fabric seemed to be covered with scatters of starlight. The low-cut bodice promised to reveal more than she ever had before, while the slender skirt would outline her hips and legs. It was a sensual garment for a sophisticated woman. Phoebe wasn't sure she had the courage to wear it.

A note fluttered to the floor. She set the dress back in the box and picked up the folded paper.

She recognized the strong, masculine handwriting instantly. Besides, who but Mazin would be sending her a dress?

"I know you will try to refuse my gift," he wrote. "You may even call me names and chide me for my boldness. I could not face your temper—for the thought of your anger leaves me trembling with fear. So I am leaving this dress in secret, like a thief in the night."

Phoebe knew she couldn't possibly accept such an extravagant gift. However, Mazin's note made her smile and then laugh. As if anything about her could ever frighten him.

She made the mistake of carrying the dress over to the mirror and holding it up in front of herself. Then she tried it on.

As she'd feared, the sensual fabric clung to every curve. Yet something about the material or the style or both made her actually look as if she *had* something worth clinging to. Her breasts seemed fuller, her waist smaller. She had a vision of herself in more dramatic makeup, with her hair cascading in curls down her back. While she'd never believed that she looked anything like Ayanna, with a little help she might come close.

Still wearing the dress, Phoebe dashed for the phone. She called the beauty salon in the hotel. Luckily they had a cancellation and would be happy to assist her in her transformation. If she would care to come downstairs in a half hour or so?

Phoebe agreed and hung up. Then she returned her attention to her reflection. Tonight she would look like the best possible version of herself. Would it be enough?

Phoebe arrived first at the restaurant. Mazin had called at the last minute, telling her that he was delayed with a small matter of work. He had sent a car to collect her and had promised to join her by seven.

She was shown to a private table upstairs. Carved screens kept the curious from knowing who sat there, while allowing her a perfect view of the stage. A cluster of musicians sat on one side of the room playing for the diners. Candlelight twinkled from every table.

The waiter lingered for several minutes, talking and staring until Phoebe realized he thought she was attractive. She'd never captured a man's attention before, and while the appreciative gleam in the young man's eyes flattered her, there was only one opinion that mattered.

The waiter disappeared for a few minutes, then returned with champagne. He poured her a glass. When he would have lingered longer, she told him she would be fine by herself. Obviously disappointed by the dismissal, he left.

Phoebe sipped the bubbly liquid. To think that after nearly three short weeks on the island a young man had actually noticed her. Much of it was the dress and the makeover, she thought, knowing she had never looked better. But she suspected there was some other reason. She was a different person than she had been when she arrived on the island.

Being with Mazin had changed her.

She leaned back in her chair. Except for the occasional afternoon when he'd had to return to work or his family, Mazin had spent most of his days with her. They had talked about everything from history to books to movies to her youth to her plans when she returned to Florida. They had shared sunsets, meals, laughter and he had been more than kind the few times she had given in to tears. They had been to every place on Ayanna's list. Every place but one. Lucia's Point.

Phoebe took a deep breath to calm her suddenly frantic nerves. She had little time left on the island, and then she would return to her small, solitary world. She knew that being with Mazin was a once-in-a-lifetime experience, but when she was home things would go on as before. She would attend college and get her degree in nursing. Perhaps she would do better at making friends, perhaps she might even meet a young man. But there, no one would ever be as much a part of her as Mazin. Wherever she went and whatever she did, he would be with her.

She knew that their time together hadn't meant the same thing to him as it did to her, and she could accept that. But she liked to think that she mattered a little. He had indicated that he found her attractive, that he enjoyed kissing her. So she had to ask.

Maybe he would laugh. Maybe he would be embarrassed and try to refuse her gently. Perhaps she had completely misunderstood his interest. But regardless of the many possibilities for rejection, she would not have regrets.

Voices in the hallway distracted her. She turned and saw Mazin slipping between the screens. He was as tall and handsome as ever. The black tuxedo he wore only emphasized his good looks. She rose to her feet and approached him. His smile turned from pleased to appreciative, and their kiss of greeting seemed as natural as breathing.

"I see you are wearing the dress I sent you. I trust you will not punish me for my boldness."

His teasing made her smile. In that moment her heart tightened in her chest, giving her a little tug. Phoebe had the sudden realization that she was in more danger than she had thought. Had she already fallen in love with Mazin?

Before she could consider the question, the pace of the music increased. Several young women took to the stage and began to dance. Phoebe and Mazin were seated and the waiter appeared with their first course.

Something about the rapid movement of the dancers captured Phoebe's attention. Part of it might have been that it was safer to look at them than gaze at Mazin. Apprehension made it impossible for her to eat.

"Some dances are for entertainment," he said, leaning close to be heard. She could inhale the masculine fragrance of him, and the appealing scent made her tremble. "Some tell a story. This is the journey of the nomads in their search for water. The life-giving force is essential."

He continued talking, but she couldn't listen to anything but the thundering of her heart. Could she do this? Could she not? Would she rather ask and know, or would she rather wonder? Hadn't Ayanna made her promise not to have regrets?

"You have yet to touch your food, and I suspect you are not listening to me."

She turned to him. The beat of the music seemed to thunder in her blood.

She studied his face, the way his dark hair had been brushed back from his forehead, the strong cut of his cheekbones, the faint bow in his top lip.

He touched her face with his knuckles. "Tell me, Phoebe. I can see the questions in your eyes, and something that looks like fear. Yet you need not fear anything from me. Surely we have spent enough hours together for you to know that."

"I *do* know," she whispered, unable to look away from his compelling gaze. "It's just…" She drew in a breath. "You have been more than kind to me. I want you to know that I appreciate all you've done."

He smiled. "Do not thank me too heartily. Kindness was not my motivation. I'm far too selfish a man for that."

"I don't believe that. Nor do I understand what you see in me. I'm young and inexperienced. But you've made everything about my time here really wonderful. So it seems wrong to ask for one more thing.''

''Ask me for anything. I suspect I will find it difficult to refuse you.''

He brushed his thumb across her lower lip. She shivered. The contact made her want so much, and it also, along with his words, gave her courage.

''Mazin, would you take me to Lucia's Point tomorrow?''

His dark eyes turned unreadable. Not by a flicker of a lash did he give away what he was thinking. She swallowed.

''I know the custom. That I may only go there with a lover. I don't have one. A lover, I mean. I've never...'' Why didn't the man say something? She could feel herself blushing. Words began to fail her. ''I thought you might like to stay with me tonight. To change that. To—''

Her throat closed and she had to stop talking. Unable to meet his gaze any longer, she stared at her lap and waited for him to start laughing.

Mazin studied the young woman in front of him. He had always thought of her as a quiet beauty, but tonight she was the most beautiful creature he had ever seen. Some of her transformation came from the dress and makeup, but much of it was the result of a subtle confidence. At last Phoebe didn't doubt herself.

Until she had asked him to be her lover. He read the uncertainty in her posture, the questions in the quiver of her mouth. He knew she was unaware of how much he desired her, nor would she understand the iron control it had taken for him to keep his distance. Even as they sat there, his arousal pulsed painfully. If she had any experience, she would not question her appeal. But she did not possess that kind of worldliness.

He supposed a better man would find a way to refuse her gently. He knew he was the wrong person to take the precious gift she offered. For the first time in his life, he did not feel worthy.

Yet he could not find it in his heart to walk away. He had wanted her for too long. The need inside him burned. To be her first, to hold her and touch her and make her his own—no one had ever offered him more.

"My dove," he murmured, leaning close.

She raised her head, her eyes brimming with tears. Doubt clouded her pretty features. He brushed away a few tears that spilled over, then kissed her mouth.

"I have ached for you from the moment I first saw you," he said, speaking the absolute truth. "If I do not have you, a part of me will cease to exist."

Her mouth curved into a smile. "Is that a yes?"

He laughed. "It is."

There would be consequences. To make love with a mature woman of experience was one thing—to take a virgin to his bed was another. Honor was at stake. Perhaps in this modern time there were those who took such things lightly, but not him. Not with Phoebe.

He wondered what she would say if he told her the truth. Would she still want him in her bed? His conscience battled briefly with the notion of telling her. But he needed her too much to risk it.

He shifted so he could speak directly into her ear.

"Tell me of your appetites," he murmured. "Would you like to stay for the rest of the meal and watch the dancers? Lingering will increase the anticipation. Or do you prefer to adjourn now?"

"I don't want to wait."

Her simple words sent a bolt of desire through him. His arousal ached. Tonight would be both endless torture and ultimate pleasure. He was determined to show her all the possibilities and make her first time as perfect as possible. Assuming his need did not kill him first.

## *Chapter 7*

They left the restaurant immediately. Phoebe tried not to be scared as they stood waiting for Mazin's car. But instead of his usual Mercedes, a black limo pulled up.

"I wanted tonight to be special," he said with a smile as he helped her into the back seat. "I thought you would enjoy the change."

She'd never been in a limo before, but saying that would make her sound even more unworldly and innocent than she was. Instead she tried to smile her thanks, even though her mouth didn't seem to want to cooperate.

Her brain was a complete blank. The drive back to the hotel would be about fifteen minutes. Obviously they had to talk about something, but she couldn't come up with a subject. What exactly was one supposed to discuss before making love for the first time?

She glanced frantically around the luxurious interior. The seats were camel color, and the softest leather she had ever touched. To the left was a complicated entertainment center with dozens of dials, levers and switches, along with a small television. To the right was a full bar. A bottle of champagne sat in an ice bucket.

"Had you already planned on us..." Her voice trailed off.

Mazin followed her gaze and touched the bottle of champagne. "I had thought we might take a walk along the beach and enjoy the moonlight," he said. "But I had not hoped to have the honor of doing more than kissing you. If I had, I would have been more prepared."

*More* prepared? Was that possible? Didn't the limo and the champagne spell seduction? Had her invitation simply made things easier for him?

She wanted to ask Mazin, but he was no longer paying attention to her. Instead he seemed to be searching for something. He ran his hands along the back of the seat and pressed against the wood paneling on the doors.

"What are you looking for?" she asked, bewildered.

"There is a storage compartment somewhere." He shifted to the seat behind the driver and examined the leather.

"My oldest son mentioned it to me," he said, more to himself than to her. "He joked about always keeping the car stocked."

Phoebe had no idea what he was talking about. She assumed he meant the older of his four boys, the one away at college.

"Why would your son be using a limo?"

Mazin didn't answer. He pressed against the wood panel. "At last," he said as it gave way.

The paneling opened to reveal a good-sized compartment. There was a change of clothing, more champagne and a box that she couldn't quite see. Mazin reached for the box. She shrank back into the corner of the seat when she read the labeling.

Condoms.

Phoebe's romantic images of what might happen that evening crashed in around her. Reality was not a fuzzy, slow-motion dance of kissing and touching. If they were going to make love, then there were potential consequences of the act. Protection was required. The sensible part of her brain applauded Mazin's sensible nature. Her romantic heart shriveled inside.

He glanced up and saw her. She was unable to turn away before he had a chance to see the expression on her face. She didn't know what she looked like, but whatever it was, it was enough to make him swear under his breath.

He shoved several packets into his tux pocket, closed the compartment and returned to her side.

"You do not want me to be practical?" he asked, putting an arm around her and pulling her close.

"I know it's important." She stared at the crisp edge of his collar rather than at his face. "I appreciate you taking care of me by, um, you know. Making sure you had, ah, protection."

"But it has destroyed the fantasy, yes?"

She raised her gaze to his face. "How did you know what I was thinking?"

"I know you, my dove. I promise to make this night as fantastical as I know how, but I will not compromise your health or leave you with something you did not want."

A baby. He was talking about her getting pregnant. In that second, Phoebe desperately wanted to have his child. What she would give to have a little girl with his dark, flashing eyes and easy grace. Or a sturdy little boy like Dabir, who fearlessly took on the world.

He touched her chin, forcing her to raise her head, then he bent and kissed her.

The soft pressure of his lips chased away her doubts. He kept the kiss light, but just being close to him was enough to make her body tingle all over. Before she could tempt him to deepen the contact, the car stopped.

She raised her head. "Where are we?"

"A side entrance to the hotel," he said, opening the door and stepping out into the night. "I did not think you would be comfortable walking with me to the elevator. At this time of night the lobby would be crowded.''

''Thank you,'' she said as she followed him down a flower-lined path to a glass door that led in from the garden.

Trust Mazin to be so considerate. She would have been embarrassed to have everyone know what they were going upstairs to do.

Once inside, he led her to a service elevator in the back and they arrived on her floor without being seen by anyone. She fumbled for her key until he took her small evening bag from her and removed it. Then he unlocked the door and drew her inside her room.

The balcony door stood open. A single lamp on the nightstand burned, and housekeeping had already been by to turn down the bed. Phoebe could smell the scent of the sea. She told herself to focus on that and not on her jangling nerves.

Mazin locked the door and set her purse on the table by the mirror. He crossed to stand in front of her.

''I see your tension has returned,'' he said lightly. ''Feel it if you must. But feel this as well.'' He pressed his mouth to her throat.

The warm, damp kiss made her legs go weak. She had to hold on to him to keep from sliding to the floor. He kissed her neck, and licked the sensitive skin by her ear. One of his hands rested on her shoulder, his fingers rubbing her bare skin.

''Beautiful Phoebe,'' he breathed before taking her earlobe into his mouth and nibbling.

Goose bumps broke out on her skin as he shifted to stand behind her. Her breasts seemed to swell as her nipples tightened. Between her legs she felt a tension and an ache that made her want to press herself against him.

He moved her hair over her shoulder and kissed his way down the back of her neck, to her shoulder blades. She hadn't thought of her back as a very erotic part of her body, but when he lightly stroked her there, and followed that contact by an openmouthed kiss, she found it difficult to breathe.

As he nibbled on her shoulder, he ran his hands up and down her arms. From there he slid his fingers to her waist. Anticipation filled her as he circled slowly, climbing higher and higher. He stood behind her and kissed her neck, even as he moved his hands up to touch her breasts.

She exhaled in wonder as he cupped her small curves, holding them in his hands as if they were most precious cargo. Even through the material of the dress she felt his warmth and the tender way he moved against her sensitized flesh.

The style of the dress was such that she couldn't wear a bra—at least, not any one that she had. At first she'd been nervous about going out that way, but now, with him stroking her, she was grateful. One less layer between his fingers and her aching body.

She loved how he explored her curves. She wanted

to beg him to slip off her dress so she could know what it was like to have him touch her bare skin. She wanted—

She gasped as he lightly touched her nipples. She'd known they were tight with desire, but she hadn't realized how sensitive that puckered skin could be. Fire shot through her, racing along her arms and legs before settling deep in her belly. He brushed against them again and again, making her groan and lean back against him as pleasure filled her.

She wasn't sure how long they stood there, him touching her, her savoring the contact. At last he turned her in his arms and kissed her. A deep, satisfying kiss that made her body melt and her toes curl. She wrapped her arms around him, wanting to be as close as possible. This was what she'd waited for all her life. Nothing could go wrong as long as Mazin continued to touch her.

She felt the slide of the zipper being pulled down in back. Cool evening air tingled against her bare skin. She wore panties, a garter belt and stockings under her dress. Nothing more. The ladies in the boutique had insisted on the latter when they'd seen her dress, telling her that regular panty hose would be a crime under such a beautiful gown. Phoebe hadn't been sure, but as Mazin pushed her dress off her shoulders and she thought of how she looked underneath, she was glad she had let them convince her.

The dress fell to the floor. She was close enough to him that she wasn't yet embarrassed about being practically naked. His large, warm hands moved up and down her back, touching her, soothing her, arousing her until she longed for him to do more. Then he slipped lower—to her hips and the garter belt there. And lower, to the high-cut panties, the bare skin of her thigh, then to the tops of the stockings. He froze.

Mazin broke the kiss and stared at her. Fire seemed to radiate from his dark eyes and tension pulled his mouth straight.

"I want you," he breathed.

There was nothing he could have said that was more perfect. The last of Phoebe's fears faded. She leaned forward and kissed him. It was the first time she had initiated any contact. She licked his lower lip, then nipped at the full flesh. He grabbed her and pulled her close, deepening the kiss with an intensity that convinced her he was a man in great need of a woman.

She felt something hard pressing against her belly. His arousal, she thought, happy to know that she could affect him so. She wanted to explore her new and wondrous power over him when he moved his hands to her waist.

The feel of them on bare skin was very different than the feel of them through her dress. She moved back so he could move higher. He didn't disappoint her. He slipped up to cup her breasts, then touched her nipples with his thumbs.

She hadn't known there was that much pleasure in the world. Her mind faded to blackness and she could only experience what he was doing to her. She wasn't even aware of pulling away from the kiss until her head sagged back and she exhaled his name.

Instead of being angry, Mazin laughed softly. He bent forward, took one of her nipples in his mouth and sucked. More fire filled her. She cupped his head, running her fingers through his hair and begging him to never stop. He moved from breast to breast, back and forth, licking, blowing, caressing. Between her legs her panties grew damp. Then without warning her legs gave way.

He caught her as she fell. With an ease that surprised her, he picked her up in his arms and carried her to the bed. Her shoes got lost along the way. After standing her next to the bed, he quickly peeled off her panties, leaving her stockings in place, then eased her onto the bed.

Phoebe had a brief flash of panic, but before it could take hold, he was next to her, holding her, kissing her. He rested his hand on her breast, which made her forget everything bad and think only of how he made her feel.

When he moved his hand lower, he kissed her so deeply, she barely noticed. But at the first brush of his fingers against her damp curls, she found herself very aware of what he was doing.

Questions filled her mind. What was she supposed to do? What would it feel like? Before she could ask, he stroked the inside of her thigh. Without her being aware of doing anything, her legs fell open. He touched her lightly, exploring her, finding wonderful places that made her breathing quicken. He found that most secret place and slipped inside. At the same time he shifted his attention from her mouth to her breasts.

He circled her nipple, licking her sensitive skin. She didn't know what to think about—his mouth or his fingers. He withdrew from her and rubbed between her curls. Without warning, his mouth closed on her nipple and his fingers found some amazingly sensitive spot.

The combination made her forget to breathe. Not that it mattered, because whatever he was doing was too good for her to live through. She was going to die. No one could survive such pleasure. It terrified her. She never wanted it to stop.

He rubbed her gently, moving faster and faster. Suddenly she was breathing again, or rather gasping. She rolled her head back and forth as pressure built.

"Mazin?"

"Hush, my dove. I am here."

And then he was kissing her and touching her and the world began to spin. There was a final push within her, a pinnacle of pressure, and then the most glorious release. She clung to him, shaking, trembling, hungry and satisfied, all at the same time.

When it was over, he drew her close, kissing her face and making her feel as if she were the most precious creature on earth.

"I didn't know," she whispered. "That's pretty amazing."

He stared into her eyes. "There is so much more I long to show you."

"I'd like that."

He sat up and pulled off his coat and shirt. Shoes and socks followed, then trousers. When he was naked, she raised herself up on one elbow to study him. The sight of his body pleased her. She watched as he slipped on the condom, then parted her legs for him.

He waited to enter her, first kissing her and touching her everywhere until that unbelievable pleasure built up to the point of nearly exploding. Just when she was about to go over the edge, he pushed inside her.

Her body stretched to take him. The pressure was uncomfortable at first, then eased. He reached between them and touched that one perfect spot. The feel of him inside her while he stroked her sent her higher and higher. She could barely hold on.

He shifted so that he could wrap his arms around her and kiss her. The change in their positions forced his arousal in deeper. She clung to him. Everything was so unfamiliar, yet so right, and she lost herself on the next thrust. She called out his name even as he shuddered and clung to her.

She opened her eyes. Mazin stared at her. Even as her climax washed over her and his ripped through him, they gazed at each other. It was a moment of intimate connection, far beyond anything she'd ever experienced. In that moment, she knew the truth. That no matter how far she traveled from this magical paradise, no matter who she met or what she experienced, she would only ever love one man.

Mazin.

# Chapter 8

Phoebe awoke just before dawn. An unfamiliar weight draped around her waist and it took her a second to realize it was Mazin's arm. She smiled and snuggled closer to him.

"Good morning," he whispered in her ear. He lay behind her, his body warm and welcoming against her own. "How are you feeling?"

"Pretty darned perfect," she said happily.

Something hard poked into the back of her leg. She giggled. "I didn't realize that people could make love so often," she said.

"I assure you that four times in a night is not usual. You inspire me." He withdrew a little. "However, this is new to you, so I will restrain myself."

She thought about how one of the times he hadn't entered her at all. He'd kissed her intimately until she'd been unable to keep from losing herself in the glory of his attentions. He'd then taught her how to pleasure him that way. As he had promised, there was much to explore.

He glanced at the clock and groaned. "I must return home for a short time, my dove. I have breakfast with Dabir each morning and I would not want to explain my absence. But I will return in a few hours and we can make our way to Lucia's Point." He leaned over and kissed her. "There in the shadow of the waterfall I will make love with you."

She melted at the thought.

He rose and quickly dressed, then kissed her again before leaving. "Miss me," he said. "As I will miss you."

"Always," she promised, and knew it was the truth.

The sound of the waterfall made it nearly impossible to speak. Phoebe stood, transfixed by the sight of so much water tumbling from nearly a hundred feet in the air. A fine mist cooled her bare arms and face. She leaned back in Mazin's arms.

This was, she thought contentedly, a perfect moment. Last night she had learned what it meant to be loved by a man. Over and over Mazin had touched her, kissed her and taken her to paradise. With practice, she would learn to seduce *him*. She wanted that. She wanted to make him ache with longing. She wanted to make him tremble and hunger so that he couldn't hold back any longer.

She wanted to make him love her.

Phoebe sighed quietly. Love. Could a man like Mazin ever care about her? She was young and didn't share his life experiences. He was worldly and wealthy. She hadn't even been to college. They had very little in common. And yet…in her heart, being with him felt so very right. Now, in his embrace, she knew that she had come home. How could her feelings be so strong without him having the same reaction? Was it possible for her to love so deeply and have him completely unaffected?

"What are you thinking?" he asked, speaking the question directly in her ear.

"That the falls are very beautiful. Are we really going to make love here?"

He turned her in his arms and kissed her. She recognized the passion flaring in his eyes. "Do not doubt my desire for you, my dove," he said, taking her hand and placing it on his arousal.

He was already hard. She wrapped her arms around him. "Oh, Mazin."

"Yes. Speak my name," he murmured against her mouth. "Know only me."

He undressed her slowly, peeling away layers of clothing until she was naked on the blanket he'd brought with them. Sunlight shone through the leaves overhead, creating changing patterns of shadows on her legs and torso. Mazin undressed himself, then joined her on the ground. As he kissed her deeply and touched her breasts, she felt herself melting inside.

Heat filled her. Dampness signaled her readiness. When he stroked her intimately, she shuddered in preparation of her release.

He took her to the edge and when she would have slipped off into paradise, he drew back enough to ease her on top of him. The unfamiliar position felt awkward at first, but she soon saw the advantages of controlling his rhythm inside her. While she moved up and down on his maleness, he cupped the apex of her thighs and rubbed his thumb against her tiny place of pleasure. Tension made her shudder. Need made her cry out.

She lost control there in the warm sunlight, with the thunder of the falls in the background. The soft call of birds provided romantic music for their lovemaking. He shuddered beneath her, losing himself as well, calling out her name, making her feel as if she'd finally found her place to belong.

"We must talk," he said later, when they were dressed and walking back to his car. "There is something I haven't told you."

Phoebe didn't like the sound of that. She shivered, as if the sun had disappeared behind a cloud. Was he going to tell her that their time together was over?

"I don't want to talk," she said quickly. "I'm leaving in a few days. Can't we keep these happy memories alive until then?"

He sighed. "Phoebe, I do not mean to frighten you. I am not trying to end our relationship—I simply seek to change it. But before I do that, I must tell you the truth about myself."

She climbed into the car. Where before her flesh had tingled with anticipation, now her skin simply felt cold. She wanted to wrap herself in the blanket Mazin had brought. Except it carried the sweet fragrance of their lovemaking, and if she inhaled that, she would cry. She was determined that regardless of what Mazin said, she would not cry. She would be strong and mature and brave. She owed that to herself, if not to him.

She waited until he slid behind the wheel, then stared straight out the front windshield.

''You're married.''

He turned to stare at her. ''I told you, my wife died six years ago. I have not remarried. For a time I had thought I would take another wife, but finding someone seemed an impossible task. I gave up the idea.''

He started the engine. ''I am doing this badly. Perhaps rather than telling you, I should show you. I want—'' He hesitated. ''Most women would be pleased, but I am not sure of your reaction.''

If he was trying to make her feel better, he was doing a lousy job. Phoebe bit her bottom lip as he drove them toward the coast road, and then headed north. Part of her wanted to hear what he had to say, because if he told her to her face that their relationship was over, then eventually she would be able to stop loving him. At least, that would be her plan. But if she ran away, she might never get over him. Although the thought of disappearing back into her hotel and not coming out until it was time for her flight had a certain appeal.

She was lost in her thoughts and didn't notice they'd begun to drive up to the top of the island until she recognized the road to the palace. Her throat tightened, making it impossible to swallow.

"Mazin, why are we here?"

He didn't say anything. Her mind began to race, and not in a good way. Various possibilities occurred to her and she wasn't sure she liked any one of them.

Instead of stopping in front of the palace, he kept driving down a road that led to a large building. One he'd pointed out to her before. The private residence of the prince.

Her entire world shifted slightly. Her brain froze, her heart stopped beating for a second, then began again but this time at a thunderous pace. And before either of them could speak, a small child broke through a grove and ran toward the car.

Mazin slowed, then pulled to the edge of the road. When he parked, Dabir ran to her side of the car and pulled open her door.

"Did you ask her? Did she say yes?"

"Dabir, we have discussed nothing," Mazin growled, although his son didn't seem the least bit impressed by his temper. "We need more time."

"But you've had all morning," the boy complained. "Did you tell her that I think she's pretty? Did you tell her about being a princess?"

"Dabir!"

Mazin's voice echoed through the trees. Dabir squeaked, then grinned. "Say yes, Miss Carson. Please?" he pleaded, then took one look at his father and headed back the way he'd come. The sound of his laughter drifted to them.

Phoebe didn't know what to say or what to think. She felt as if she'd fallen into an alternative universe. "M-Mazin?"

He sighed. "This is not what I had planned. We are sitting in a car. It is not romantic." He released his seat belt and angled toward her. "Phoebe, what I have not told you is that I am more than a minister in the Lucia-Serrat government. I am Crown Prince Nasri Mazin. I rule this island. The house before us is my home. My sons are princes."

She blinked several times. C-crown p-prince Nasri Mazin? Even her thoughts stuttered. "No," she whispered. "You can't be."

He shrugged. "Yet I am."

She stared at his familiar face, at the dark eyes and firm mouth. The mouth she'd kissed and that had kissed her back in many very intimate places. Heat flared on her cheeks. "But I've seen you naked!"

He grinned. "Yes. As I have seen you."

She didn't want to think about that. "I don't understand. If you're really a prince, why didn't you tell me? And why did you want to be with me?"

He brushed a strand of hair from her face. "When I met you at the airport, I had recently returned from an extended journey. In the back of my mind had been the thought that I should find a wife. I did not expect to marry for love, but I thought I would find a woman with whom I could enjoy life. But that was not to be. The women I met bored me. I grew tired of them wanting me for my position or my money. I came home weary and discouraged."

He shrugged. "Then I saw a pretty young woman walk into the duty-free shop. She looked fresh and charming and very unlike the other women I'd been seeing. I followed her on an impulse. That same impulse caused me to speak with her. She had no idea who I was. At first I thought her innocence was a game, but in time I discovered it was as genuine as the young woman herself. I was intrigued."

She still wasn't thinking straight. In fact, she wasn't thinking at all. "But Mazin…" She swallowed. "I mean Prince Nasri—" She squeezed her eyes shut. This couldn't be happening to her.

A prince? She'd fallen in love with a prince? Which meant any teeny, tiny hopes she'd had about a happily ever after had just disappeared like so much smoke.

"Phoebe, do not look so sad."

She opened her eyes and stared at him. "I'm not. I feel foolish, which is different. I should have guessed."

"I went to great pains to see that you did not. I arranged our travels in advance, making sure there wouldn't be anyone around."

And here she'd just thought it was the slow season. She'd been a fool. "I guess no one is going to believe me if I try to tell them this when I get back home."

"Ayanna would have believed," he said softly.

She nodded. Ayanna would have understood everything, she thought with a sigh. Because the same sort of thing had happened to her aunt. And Ayanna had spent the rest of her life loving the one man she could never have.

Pain tightened her chest, making it difficult to breathe. "You should, ah, probably take me back to the hotel now," she murmured.

"But I have not answered your second question."

She wasn't sure how much longer she could sit there without crying. "W-what question is that?"

"You asked to know why I wanted to be with you."

Oh. She didn't think she wanted to hear that answer. It couldn't be good. Or at least not good enough.

He put his hands on her shoulders. "You enchanted me. I do not get the opportunity to meet many people without them knowing I am Prince Nasri of Lucia-Serrat. With you, I could be myself. When you told me about your aunt's list of places to go, I decided to show them to you. I wanted to spend time with you. To get to know you."

That wasn't so bad. She forced herself to smile. "I appreciate all you've done. You were very kind."

He shook her gently. "Do you think kindness was my sole purpose?"

Why was he asking such hard questions? "I thought, maybe, after a while, you might want to seduce me."

Mazin groaned, then leaned forward and kissed her on the mouth. "Yes, I wanted you in my bed, but it was more than that," he said between kisses. "I wanted to be with you. I could not forget you. You became very important to me. I did not plan for you to meet my son, but that turned out to be most fortuitous. Dabir thinks you are very lovely and that you would make an excellent mother."

If the world had tilted before, it positively spun now, swooping and zooming around her until she found it impossible to keep her balance. Her fingers shook as she unfastened her seat belt, then stumbled out of the car. She was going to faint. Worse, she thought she might be sick.

Mazin…make that Prince Nasri…hurried around the car to stand next to her. "Phoebe? What's wrong?"

"You want me to take Nana's place?"

No. That wasn't possible. She couldn't stay here and take care of Mazin's child, all the while watching him with other women. She would be destroyed. Even if her heart weren't a consideration, she had her own dreams and they didn't involve her staying on Lucia-Serrat as a nanny.

Suddenly he was in front of her, grabbing her by her upper arms and shaking her gently. "Is that what you believe?" He stared at her face, then shook his head and pulled her close. "Don't you know I love you, you little fool? What did you think? That I wanted to hire you as a caretaker to my child? I have that for Dabir already. What I do not have is a mother for him and a wife for myself. I do not have a woman to love—someone to love me in return."

She stepped back and looked at him. His words filled her brain, but she couldn't grasp them. "I don't understand."

"Obviously."

And then he kissed her.

His warm, tender mouth settled on hers. As he wrapped his arms around her, she allowed herself to believe that he might have been telling the truth.

"You love me?" she asked, breathless, but with a little less heart pain.

"Yes, my dove. I suspect nearly from the first."
He stroked her hair, then her cheek. "For many years
now I have been disenchanted with my life. Everything felt wrong. I loved my sons, but they could not
completely fill my heart. I have traveled everywhere
and never felt at home, until I met you. When I saw
my island through your eyes, it was as if I had seen
it for the first time. Your gentle strength, your honest
heart, your giving spirit touched me and healed me. I
have searched the world only to find my heart's desire
standing right in front of me."

He kissed her again. "Marry me, Phoebe. Marry
me and stay here. Be mother to my sons, be princess
to my people. But most of all, love me always, as I
will love you."

"A p-princess?"

He smiled. "It's a very small island. Your duties
would not be taxing."

"I wouldn't mind the work. I just never imagined
anything like this."

"Will you say yes?"

She gazed into his dark eyes. She didn't care that
he was a prince. What mattered to her was that he
was the man she loved. This wasn't *her* dream…it
was something much bigger and better. It was her
heart's desire.

"Yes."

He drew her close and hugged her as if he would
never let her go. "For always," he promised. "We
will live life to the fullest, with no regrets. Just as
your Ayanna would have wanted."

# LOOK OUT...

...for this month's special product offer.
It can be found in the envelope
containing your invoice.

**Special offers are exclusively for
Mills & Boon® Book Club members.**

You will benefit from:

- Free books & discounts
- Free gifts
- Free delivery to your door
- No purchase obligation – 14 day trial
- Free prize draws

THE LIST IS ENDLESS!!

*So what are you waiting for —
take a look* **NOW!**

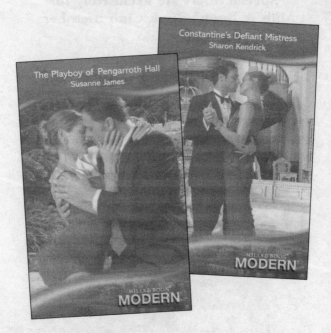

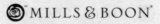

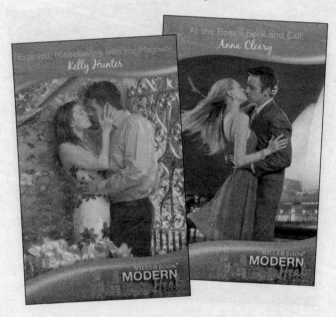

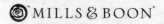